Percy H. Fitzgerald

Puppets

Vol. I

Percy H. Fitzgerald

Puppets
Vol. I

ISBN/EAN: 9783337066185

Printed in Europe, USA, Canada, Australia, Japan

Cover: Foto ©Andreas Hilbeck / pixelio.de

More available books at **www.hansebooks.com**

A Romance

BY

PERCY FITZGERALD

AUTHOR OF " BELLA DONNA," " NEVER FORGOTTEN."

> " See how the merry puppets dance !
>   You think it's all their little will ;
>   But though they frisk, and though they prance,
>   They are but merry puppets still."

IN THREE VOLUMES.—VOL. I.

LONDON: CHAPMAN AND HALL

LIMITED

1884

Bungay:
CLAY AND TAYLOR, PRINTERS.

CONTENTS OF VOL. I.

Prologue.

CHAPTER I.

CHAPTER II.

CHAPTER III.

CHAPTER IV.

CHAPTER V.

CHAPTER VI.

CHAPTER VII.

CHAPTER VIII.

CHAPTER I.

CHAPTER II.

CHAPTER III.

CHAPTER IV.

CHAPTER V.

CHAPTER VI.

CHAPTER VII.

CHAPTER XVI.

CHAPTER XVII.

CHAPTER XVIII.

PUPPETS.

PROLOGUE.

CHAPTER I.

MR. BENBOW'S THOUGHTS IN DIPCHESTER CHURCH.

As a ray of the morning's sunlight fell aslant
on the family pew one brilliant Sunday morning in Dipchester church, it lit up the face—a
rather notable one — of Mr. Spencer Pelham
Benbow, the chief personage in the parish. That
sunlight seemed of a complimentary sort, and
imparted a genial air of festival to the service
going on in the old church. For beside him sat,
as was well known to every member of the
congregation, an unassuming-looking gentleman,
of Bank-director-like aspect; and next him an

elegantly-dressed, cold-looking lady, his daughter. Behind, in the roomy pew, which was like the cabin of a brig, and had a stove, were "supernumeraries"—those . undistinguished rank and file of visitors to a country house. The service seemed to be conducted with extra reverence and devotion, and every face in the congregation was periodically turned to the pew with an unusual awe. It was well known that these unobtrusive strangers were no other than the Duke of Banff-shire and his daughter, the Lady Rosa, now on a visit at Benbow Towers. "A real live Duke," said the simple rustics to each other: such a visitation was not remembered within the memory of man.

It might be speculated, in what place would the ancestral trophies and associations of a family, their friends, neighbours, and general position, be best and most conveniently brought together? Not at the Heralds' College, nor in the Muniment Room, or even in the family pic-ture-gallery: but perhaps in the village church, of a Sunday—so old, and whitened, with its bottle-green diamond panes all bent and wavy. There, with a whispering sexton or pew-opener at his ear, the careless stranger, dropping in for a few moments, would have the living figures themselves before him, as well as the records of the dead upon the walls; the neighbours grouped round, and the whole parish in force.

It is thus that one would best know Mr. Benbow of Benbow Towers. There he is, sitting in his pew, thinking of his illustrious companion the Duke, and of his daughter the Lady Rosa, rather than of the words of the monotonous preacher.

Dipchester church, in which his busy mind muses and travels away swiftly to London—to ministers' cabinets, to the future, to the past—is too familiar to disturb him now. Yet it is often that an accident will settle the thoughts on an object that has been before the eyes, and never seriously noticed before. Over his head was a " fine mural tablet," with a sad, bewailing inscription, to the memory of one Edmund Spencer Benbow, Esq., who must have died a saint, from the glowing terms of his inscription

—the present Mr. Benbow's father. Near him a sculptured urn, and unanimated bust, with a broken sword and helmet. Underneath an inscription, also of the most extravagantly-complimentary sort, to "Colonel Edward Benbow," son of the above, and the other's eldest son, to whom had succeeded the present Mr. Benbow, the present incumbent of the pew. But there was a yet more magnificent tomb, with mosaics and carvings :

Sacred to the Memory

OF

EDWD. HENGIST BENBOW,

ONLY SON AND HEIR

OF

COLONEL EDWARD BENBOW.

HE MET HIS DEATH BY DROWNING

IN BENBOW LOCH,

AT THE EARLY AGE OF TEN YEARS.

Eheu ereptus et flebilis.

In the congregation there were plenty who knew the history of the Benbows well, and which a glance at the little boy's tomb often recalled. There was the good-natured-looking

Major Hallam, and his "soncy" plump wife—he was adjutant of the district militia; and the excellent Mrs. Winter—wife of Dr. Winter, a worthy clergyman—and mother of that before-named Mrs. Hallam. She often told the story somewhat garrulously. The incidents occurred exactly at the time of Captain Hallam's marriage with her daughter, this leading naturally enough to it. She always added at the close : "So you see what a wonderful man Spencer Benbow is, *to have lived down so much.*"

It would now be easy to see what led Mr. Benbow's thoughts, as he sat in his family pew, to the monument of the little boy. That dead boy, but for the drowning, would no doubt have been sitting where he, Mr. Benbow, sat. He would have found himself that day in some dismal suburban church in London, with his wife and children, thinking of the expenses for the coming week.

But while the wheezing organ thrums the psalm, and the preacher preaches his best, and the long service trails on, we shall also look back a few years, and call up those old images. It will not take long, and it will then be seen how he came to be seated—and unexpectedly—in the Benbow pew, and entertaining a Duke and his daughter on that memorable Sunday.

CHAPTER II.

THE Benbows were not an old family, though they had, of course, pedigree, arms, &c., exactly as though they had been old. The truth was, Mr. Benbow's grandfather had been in trade, had made a vast fortune, and had purchased Benbow Towers, " taking over " all its entire stock, traditions, pictures, and housekeeper's stories, and thus kept up the continuity of " the thing." In a couple of generations everything settled down, and, as the Americans would put it, you can " run the old family business " as effectively as though you had been there for centuries.

Nearly thirty years before, Mr. Benbow's father was living in great state and power—for he was regularly member of Parliament, almost as of right,—and exercised a haughty dominion in the district.

The eldest son was the Colonel Edward of the monument; while the second brother was the present Spencer Pelham. He was a youth wise beyond his years, thoughtful, full of generous impulses—checked, however, by a certain good sense and prudence which made him look a little coldly on the worldly schemes of his parents. For this, or some other strange reason, the latter disliked their son. He was treated from his infancy with a cold harshness and severity. The eldest was plain in face and person, awkward and retiring in his ways and habits. He did not get on with strangers, while his brother had a ready art of making his way in the world, and forming acquaintances and making friends.

This was the old, natural Spencer Benbow, altogether different from the Spencer Benbow we see on this Sunday morning seated in the church. And he would doubtless have remained as he was in those early times,—amiable, thoughtful concerning others, eager to advance his family rather than himself—but for a strange, fatal incident, which, like a Fate, overtook him without any fault of his own, and which he could not vanquish.

In this fashion both grew up. When it came to be determined what course in life each was to take, the eldest was put into the Guards, equipped with abundance of cash, and every advantage that could set him off, while his father resolved to use every means to arrange some grand and influential "match" for him— odd word, by the way, which may have been adopted from the phraseology of an horse-dealer, who looks out for a fellow to the handsome animal that is to draw his client's carriage. Nor was it creditable to the paternal feelings that this eagerness to settle his eldest in life, was in part prompted by a wish to hinder all possible chances of his second son succeeding to the estates. For this youth, for his thoughtfulness and calm deliberative characteristics, he had, strange to say, conceived a sort of dislike. One reason may have been that he felt, that with this stock of good sense, the son was likely to prove altogether independent of him, and had already indeed shown, on most occasions, that he was right when his father had been wrong. This led to a distrust and suspicion, and above all, to a curious forecast and instinct, that one day the "Town attorney," as he sometimes called him, might after all succeed to his estates. This was being perpetually whispered to him, so the next stage was a suspicion that his second son had the same idea in his head, and was calmly waiting till his time. In the aged this unreasonable suspicion takes little to grow into a something positive and certain : it is akin to the idea that your heir is impatient to succeed, and is interfering before he is entitled to do so.

Old Mr. Benbow's "right-hand man," as it is called, had been for many years one James Gordon—a smooth, clever man, devoted to the family and its interest, having been brought up on the estate. He was agent, administrator, and general director ; and lived with his wife and young family in a house near the castle, specially built for him by his patron. He too shared his employer's dislike or distrust of the second son, and not without reason, owing to a rash and foolish excess of zeal on the part of the latter. One winter, when Mr. Benbow was complaining of the falling off in some sales, or profits, his son, who was in the room, said abruptly:

"I think, father, you should know something that I have discovered by a mere accident."

"Now for something clever," said his father sarcastically; "what it is to have a wise son! Well, out with it!"

"It's my duty, father, to tell you I have found that Gordon speculates, and has lost a good deal lately."

"Well?" said his father coldly; "what is that to you?"

"Oh, nothing; save for what it is to you."

"And what is it to me, pray?"

"That is according as you look at it. I make no charge, but cannot shut my eyes to it."

"Make no charge!" said Mr. Benbow. "That's a sneaking way in which to take away an old servant's character.   I shall tell him of this calumny."

Mr. Gordon was accordingly told, and instantly begged that his accounts might be investigated. They were found correct to a shilling.   Young Benbow, however, refused to apologize, and this injured Mr. Gordon.   But he said generously that he knew Mr. Benbow's strange conduct had been dictated by the best of motives.

Nor was this young fellow, not long after, however, without his chapter of romance.   Hard-by the Benbows there lived Dr. Winter and his family.   Their house was in the green lanes of a warm and sheltered green country just outside Dipchester; it stood alone, as if it were in a vast demesne of its own, and yet it was only surrounded by a small meadow or two.   The road that led to it was a by-road.   The house was old and yet new—burly and portly, full and contented, like an old-fashioned, well-to-do gentleman, who yet went with the times, and wore as much of the modern dress as would fit him. The red of the bricks was ripe and genial.   As gig or coach drove by on the high road, the driver or passengers got a peep of crimson that warmed and comforted them. The windows were bright, and set off with fresh clean paint, and over the old roof rose a little cupola, fresh and trim, though about as antique as an old cocked-hat. Between the road and the house was a tiny lawn, with cheerful beds of scarlet geraniums flowering in huge hillocks, and a bit of balustrade that gave a hint of terrace. Such was Arbour-hill—as seen from the top of the passing coach, pronounced "an uncommon snug place" by the outsides, and where Dr. Winter, who farmed in a "jolly" way, and Mrs. Winter, and Miss Lucy Winter, the jewel of the jewel-case, lived all the year round.

Inside, it was a miracle of comfort and brightness, airy to a degree, with the old-fashioned rooms, and the quaint twist of the stairs, but with none of that old-fashionedness which brings dampness and strange unseen burrows and decay, and drifts up to a sensitive visitor sudden and unpleasant gales. And there were also alterations and additions, and the rather straitened dining-room had been expanded into a handsome modern room. It was the most comfortable and compact of places. They said to Winter, "How *did* you light on this place? Where *did* you hear of it? What would you take for the plant and good-will now, lock, stock, and barrel?" At which proposal Lucy Winter cried out in piteous protest, "Oh, papa!"

With the exception of a little girl only five or six years old, this Lucy Winter was the only child, a gay, handsome, impetuous girl of seventeen, all flash and impulse. Some one calls her from the hall as she is heard carolling above, and down she "swings" the little twisted stair, with a sort of spring, "hand-over-hand," as though she were a sailor coming down to the deck. It is a picture to see her as she stands with a little tinge of colour in her cheeks, pushing back her tossed hair, of which she had abundance of a fine honest auburn, perhaps a little rough too; and with a delightful smile of happy interrogation, says, "What is it, papa?"

This young girl had soon attracted the second son, and it was well known in the parish that the grave, thoughtful second son was deeply in love with Lucy Winter. He was not very demonstrative, but he appeared to have made it one of the settled purposes of his life that when he had made a fortune, and opened that great oyster, the world, he would return and claim her. Lucy herself seemed to accept this arrangement, as she really liked and " esteemed "—dangerous uncertain word in love's vocabulary—her admirer. All her family thought it an " excellent thing " for her to be allied to so good and sensible and amiable a youth. But who would have given that " Blue Book of a man," as some one styled him, credit for having quite a tender corner in his heart ! But this, it must be recollected, was the young Spencer Benbow of the old early days, not the Benbow of the church of the Sunday morning, who was without heart or love, or romance of any kind.

Mr. Benbow looked scornfully on this attachment, and said it was exactly what he would have expected. His second son would never raise the family. A beggar he would be, and another beggar he had found, and there would be more beggars to follow. He "washed his hands of the whole business"—a favourite hypocritical form by which the selfish convey that they had hitherto been soiling their fingers in the cause of the person thus renounced. It was noted that this sincere, honourable, manly attachment had a remarkable influence on our second son, who became more thoughtful and gracious. It should be mentioned, however, that he had "never told his love," though there had been no "preying on himself" in the shape of concealment, nothing that could suggest the "worm i'the bud."

Suddenly there appeared in the neighbourhood a certain Captain Hallam. A pleasant, off-hand, agreeable soldier, without cleverness or brilliancy but with a full stock of good-nature and good-humour, best and most "workable" of all the virtues. When we say that this officer, grown stouter and more good-humoured-looking, was seated in the church that morning, beside Lucy Winter, the train of intervening incidents may be guessed. This was the first dislocation in the character of Spencer Benbow. He had will and power sufficient to force his life to be as before, as one will force a key to turn in the obstinate wards of a lock, but at the cost of violent bendings and wrenchings.

No one knew or guessed how much that effort cost him. But he appeared to accept it all cheerfully. As for Lucy, she had given her affections for the first time, and in such a case neither logic nor pity nor feeling is thought of.

The younger son by this time saw that he could expect little or nothing from his family, whose prejudices seem to grow with years, and determined, as it is called, to go and shift for himself. There was a certain dignity in this resolution, and he hailed with pleasure the day when he would be enabled to set forth on his course independently, and earn his own living. He felt he had a taste for " business," and "affairs," and resolved to go into the city and make money for himself.

"Aye, exactly," growled his father; "just the proper thing for you to do. Go—stick a quill behind your ear."

Young Benbow parted with his family in perfect good humour, and went up to Town to seek his fortune. In a couple of years his steady character and sagacity stood in good stead. In a surprising way he made friends —rather he made himself useful to the friends he made, was helped by them because he was likely to help them, and very soon was known to be on the road to making a fortune. Old Mr. Benbow only growled more and more as this good news travelled to him.

"Low quill-driver!" he would exclaim; "I knew he'd disgrace the family."

Meanwhile Colonel Edward had been serving with his regiment, and was now ordered to Dublin. His father was now growing a little impatient, and eager that he should settle in life. Every "great house" his son was asked to, suggested the fair and noble daughter of the house; and in every letter from Mr. Benbow it was insisted that he should make haste in his selection. His son, however, took it easily enough, assuming there was no hurry He was supposed to be enjoying himself in Dublin — dancing at the Viceregal balls, and other entertainments of that gay capital.

" Ah, Ned will do well, and raise the family," his father would say, reading out one of his letters, " even though they would persuade me that all the sense has gone to the quill-driver."

There was a young dame of high degree whom his son had carelessly mentioned in one of his letters, and on this he began to build a new structure, pressing his son in every letter, and asking him " how the business was getting forward ? " " Recollect," he would say, " that our family has found you money; you must find blood and rank."

Accordingly the Colonel went on his visits to the great houses, and was received favourably by the various Lady Marys and Lady Hildas and their families.

Suddenly, one memorable Monday morning, when the Benbow post-bag had been opened, and its contents were distributed round the breakfast-table to the guests, Mr. Benbow said good-humouredly :

" Ah, the scoundrel Edward—he has written at last."

" Why, what's this— ? "

No one knew until a day later, for the paper dropped out of his grasp, and he himself fell to the floor in a fit. There was consternation and hurry, flying for doctors on horseback and in carriages. However, soon the dreadful news became known that Colonel Edward was married, and had made a " low, foolish, improvident marriage," and had nearly killed his father. There was talk of disinheriting, cutting off the entail ; for his father, who gradually recovered, full of rage and fury, was determined to slake his thirst for vengeance, and his first step was to send for " the quill-driver " from Town.

There are abundance of painful situations; but none perhaps so acute as that when an act being done in defiance of all consequences, with a sort of proud heroism, the moment arrives when the "*bill must be paid.*" There has been a faint hope that the menaces are not wholly in earnest: that finally some mode of propitiation or release will be found. But when the awful truth is disclosed that your "ships are really burnt," and that all through the rest of life the penalty must be suffered, it is to be suspected that in nearly every case the first is, a fatal unsealing of the eyes, and the despairing reflection, that what was purchased at so costly a price—was not worth the money. At least there are but few natures so heroical as to stand the shock.

The one that felt this improvident step the most was Spencer Benbow, who, strange to say, wrote a letter of sympathy to his father, saying, he felt deeply for the disappointment of what he knew had been his life's hope, and that he did not think his brother could have played so selfish a part; at the same time he begged of his father, now that the mischief was done and incurable, to make the best of it and not visit it too heavily on Edward.

Before, however, the proper steps could be taken, or indeed before the second brother could arrive, either to dissuade or mollify his father, Mr. Benbow was seized with a second fit and expired. And thus Colonel Edward Benbow, after this very narrow escape, succeeded and became Lord of the Benbows. His brother, not in the least disappointed, was eager to congratulate him. But to his astonishment the Colonel refused to see him. He was of curiously morbid and sensitive nature, inclined to see intended offence in the most harmless incidents. He had found his brother's letter among his father's papers, and naturally assumed that much more had passed, and that he had been his enemy throughout. Not long after news arrived that the new Mrs. Benbow had died—for she had been of a frail constitution.

At last undisputed Lord and owner, he did

not set himself out to look for any enjoyment in his new possessions. The place was for him accursed, and associated with two painful memories. So it was shut up, and he lived abroad, solitary and gloomy: though there was many a fair and gentle girl and dame who found him and his distress particularly interesting, and would have tried their little all to comfort him sometimes. Once or twice in the year he returned to look after his property, but he never would stay at "the Big House."

CHAPTER III.

LUCY WINTER.

At this stage a little incident of a minor sort began to flutter the parish—and this was the marriage of Captain Hallam with the fair Lucy, whom we have seen in the church on the Ducal Sunday morning.

For all this going on, as it were, while Mr. Spencer is listening abstractly to the wheezy organ, or glancing wearily to the mural tablets.

The marriage had been talked of for some years in the district, but had come about in a quiet imperceptible way. The Captain Hallam, who was to be married, had been quartered in Dipchester, the house where the marriage was to be. He had gone on foreign service, was quartered again there, and came pretty frequently, first, to get rid of ennui—afterwards, from a very natural interest, as those who saw the young girl, the precious stone of that house, could testify.

The officer was a manly, honest officer, fairly well-looking, with lively tastes and accomplishments, had good connections, and was tolerably well off in the world. All the good people of the place were sincerely glad "that the Winters had got him;" while those who were not such good Christians talked with a little depreciation of picking up a man "in a marching regiment," with only "his pay to keep himself upon."

A marriage in a country district is a great, even a tremendous, event, and the two figures become as interesting as actors upon the stage of a theatre. The gossip tongues run riot. It is like promotion to a ministerial office. Those who are looking forward to a similar advancement for their children feel something akin to envy.

When the passengers on the up-coach, going by about eight o'clock, saw the little "box" blazing cheerfully away like a bright lantern, to them it looked more than ever "snug," the very essence of snugness and warmth. If they could have drawn up the yellow blinds and peeped in, they would have seen two pictures of warmth, colour, happiness, and comfort. One was in the dining-room, with its sea-green walls, and where Mr. Trail, the grey-haired curate, and Doctor Legge, the village doctor—who, it was said, knew more of the moon and stars than of physic—and Captain Hallam, and a chosen friend and brother-officer, Hillier, who was to be his "best man," and the host, were sitting round the fire taking claret.

The ladies had just gone, had crossed the hall, and were drawing in to their fire, which makes up the other picture of warmth and comfort. Mrs. Trail and her daughter, a darling friend of Lucy's, were staying in the house. They were all drawing in closer to the fire, to continue a subject more confidentially, which had been just touched on as they left the dining-room. The subject was Colonel Benbow.

"Oh, mamma," said Lucy, "he is certain to come, he arrived at the Towers yesterday. He promised."

"I am sure he will, dear," said her mamma, "and for a reason that I know."

"But what an interesting character," said Mrs. Trail. "The world is not so bad as my dear Trail preaches, when there are men with such deep feeling as that."

"The strangest thing," said Mrs. Winter, "was their estrangement. And there can be no doubt that Spencer had spoken bitterly of his brother's behaviour to his father. And Colonel Edward always believed that but for him they would have been reconciled. When his wife died, this became a morbid, bitter dislike, which really preyed on him. But all this is an old story now, and took place some eight years ago. My dear, I could not describe it. I assure you it haunted me like a nightmare for months after. It was really terrible, his rage and grief mixed together. At times I thought his reason would go, or *had* gone. Men *can* love their wives, you see. When he lost her his grief was terrible. Since then he has wandered about the world with his son. The old grief and fury have given way, and gradually, I think, a love the most overpowering for this child—a love that is increasing every day and every hour—is softening him; and the most wonderful proof of his being softened is his coming here."

"And the boy?" asked the vicar's wife.

"A *darling!*" said Lucy, running to the table. "Look here!" And she brought over her photograph album.

In a moment they were all admiring a little fellow in a Scotch dress, leaning, his hand in his pocket, with a smile of composure—the smile of a "boy of the world"—against a very low table. He had a charming air of gracious composure. The ladies agreed he was indeed a darling.

"Now, mamma, tell Mrs. Trail what we have settled."

"Oh yes," said Mrs. Winter. "Spencer, who really never did anything in the matter, and yet was sorry, and has tried again and again to see his brother, is to be here to-morrow. He is of a cold temper though. Do you see *now?*"

"Ah, yes," said the vicar's wife. "But still, if he is in the same mood——"

"But Lucy has a plan."

"Leave it to me," said Lucy, pacing round and round the room in delight. "I have my plan, and it shall succeed. Hush!" She held up her finger. Was it the gentlemen coming in? Yes, their voices were in the hall. But Lucy heard another sound. In country houses, ears are as trained as the ears of Indian hunters, and can hear a sound of wheels on gravel even at the lodge gate.

Mrs. Winter started up. "It is Colonel Benbow!" The gentlemen came in, in delightful spirits. But Mr. Winter and his wife went out into the hall.

CHAPTER IV.

THE SON.

Through the open door, in the dark night outside, a chaise was waiting. In a moment those round the bright fire in the drawing-room heard the sound of shuffling and pattering feet. In a few minutes more the door was opened gently, and Mrs. Winter's voice was heard. " Will you come in here, Colonel Benbow ? "

A tall gentleman, with a sunburnt face and large brown moustache, and the softest of blue eyes, advanced through the doorway, and then drew back irresolutely. He held his son by the hand, who was in a dark little Scotch dress, and who looked round on all the company with a pleasant smile of greeting.

" I am afraid," began Colonel Benbow, " that after our journey——"

But he was interrupted, for, with cheeks glowing and eyes flashing, Lucy came from the other end of the room straight to him, and said :

"How are you, Colonel Edward? I am Lucy!"

He half started back, and seemed to shade his eyes from the lamp.

"Ah, yes. I am glad to see you, dear," he said, taking her hand affectionately, "and am delighted to hear about all this. But I am ashamed coming in this way—a dusty wayworn traveller."

Every one remarked what a soft voice he had, and a gentle address, while to ladies he had a sort of reverential courtesy with a faint bloom of "old fashion" on it, but which was not the less welcome.

Mrs. Winter eagerly said these were only neighbours, and these "neighbours" with delicacy drew away, and sat in different parts of the room. But the father's eye wandered over to his son, who, having already introduced himself, was the centre of a group of ladies. He was sitting on one of the low chairs, "nursing" one of his little stockinged feet, and talking away about their journey with great volubility. He was telling them of his travels, and how he was not in the least tired. He had very delicate little features, a little nose, a pretty mouth, a fair skin, and his father's soft eyes.

"I was not in the *least* sick in the packet," he said, still nursing his little leg. "I *never am—* neither I nor papa. There was a French child, though. You should have seen *him!*" And the little fellow laughed and crowed over the abasement of the hereditary enemies of his country. "Party here to-night? Papa doesn't like parties," he went on, "*nor do I.* Do you play games here? *I* can play."

They were charmed with him; he prattled on with such composure. The captain had introduced himself, not with that mock respect and burlesque "humbugging" with which young men "draw out" children, and whom they use merely to show themselves off.

"How d'ye do?" said the boy graciously.

" I am very glad to have the pleasure of know-ing you. Would you tell me, please," and he hesitated a little, " who the lady is, over there, that you were talking with ? "

The captain laughed. " Oh, that is the prettiest, finest young lady in the world. At least *I* think so."

" Not in the world," said the boy, shaking his head gravely. " Because you have not seen *all* the young ladies in the world. But still—oh yes, she is very pretty."

" Then why are you so curious about all this, Master Benbow ? I declare I am beginning to be a little jealous."

" Ah," said the boy, quickly, " you are going to marry her ? "

" Yes, you have guessed it," said the captain. " Am I not a happy fellow ? "

" Indeed I think so," said the boy, swinging one leg, and in the same wistful sincere way. " She is very nice—much nicer than the French ladies."

Lucy came running over.

"Here she is herself," said the captain, gaily ; and then added, in a half whisper, "I won't tell her what you said—about her not being the finest and prettiest young lady in the world."

"I didn't mean *that*," said the boy, colouring, and stepping back with a little defiance; "you know I would not say so."

Lucy was down on her knees, holding his hands and looking into his face. "What is it that you don't mean, dear?" she asked. "Tell *me*—we are to be the greatest friends."

He shook his head. "No, no."

"What! You refuse me?"

"No; but you know," he said, hesitating, and still swinging on one foot—"you know you are to marry *him*, and there won't be time."

"But we shall meet afterwards," she said, still on her knees, and holding his hands, "and you must promise to come and stay with me."

"And with *him?*" asked the boy with a knowing look in his eye. "He will be the *husband*—and if he does not choose——"

"But I do choose, and always will choose—it

you will do us the honour, that is. Recollect, it is an engagement; you come very soon; I choose. Besides, whatever Lucy chooses I choose."

The boy took the hand that was held out to him, and shook it.

"The only thing," he said confidently, "is papa. He is very particular about my going anywhere by myself—that is, he does not wish that I should go anywhere without *him*. And *I* don't wish. When you come to know papa, you will like him very much. We go everywhere together. We have travelled an immense deal together, papa, and I, and Andy."

"And who is Andy, dear?" said Lucy, still on the carpet; "tell *me*."

"Bless me!" said the little fellow. "Don't you know Andy? He is our servant—our own servant"—in a confidential tone—"He came with poor dear mamma from Ireland (I never saw mamma that I can *remember*), and papa and I have *agreed* that we are never to part with Andy. Papa talks a great deal to him, but he does not like my talking much to him, as papa says I might learn to speak like Andy, who has a strong brogue. But papa says that should make no difference in his character, because he is the most faithful and trustworthy man that ever lived. And I assure you I *feel* it a good deal, not talking to Andy, because I *know* he is good. And papa means, when Andy gets old and lame, to pension him off; and, when I am grown up, I shall pension him too; for I like Andy, and should wish to be kind to him; and when you come to know him, you will like him too."

They listened to these little assurances with great pleasure, the little man was so earnest and assured. Captain Hallam looked across to Lucy with delight.

"Give me a kiss, you darling!" she said. "I like you as if I had known you from a child."

The little man put forward his cheek with great dignity.

"And I like you," he said; "and when *he* said you were the fairest young lady in the world, I did not mean to deny it—indeed no. I should not be so unpolite—no, indeed."

"Give me another kiss, you pet!" said Lucy, in great delight.

Now was heard a gentle voice calling, from the side of the room: "Now, now, take care you are not talking too much, and tiring our friends."

He walked over himself. The little man went to meet him, and took his larger hand.

"Yes, papa. Come and talk—do. Oh!"—to the little circle—"*he* can talk, papa can; you'll be *dee*-lighted."

They all smiled.

"This little fellow and I," said Colonel Edward, in his gentle, half-apologetic voice, "have been great companions. We have travelled and seen a great many things together—have we not, little man?"

"Yes, papa," said the little man, looking up at him; "and we are to see the world regularly when I get bigger—he has promised me—and I am *never* to go to school."

"Can you sing or play?" said Lucy.

"No, no," said the Colonel, a little hastily; "he will only tire you."

"Just as papa pleases," said the little man, with a bow. "Some people like my singing; others, as papa says, get tired."

"Nonsense!" cried the captain, eagerly. "Do sing for us: we shall take it as a great favour."

"Do, dear," said Lucy.

"*Would* you like it, really?" asked the little man.

"Indeed we all would, and I particularly."

"Well, papa: may I?"

"As these ladies are so kind," said the Colonel, looking round doubtfully; and he walked slowly back towards the fire, and sat down by his cousin.

Without the least shyness, the little man looked round on all the company, and began a French chanson — CADET ROUSSEL — with a burden:

> "Ah, ça! oui! vraiment!
> Cadet Roussel a trois enfans,"

and which he sang with the greatest seriousness. There was great applause when he had finished.

"Oh, I can sing other things," he said, "in quite a different style. There was one song which Andy taught me! but," he added, with sudden earnestness, "that was *long* before papa wished that I should not speak so *much* to him— it was indeed—though papa might not like it on *that* account. But, oh! it *is* such a *very* funny Irish song; and if you heard Andy sing it——"

Lucy had run over to the fireside with the request. She was whispering the Colonel.

"You won't refuse me? Let the dear boy sing. He is getting quite at home with us all. Do let him—Andy's song—do!"

The Colonel, smiling, half grave, made a protest. "For shame, little man," he said; "he picks up all these low songs; though, indeed," he added, correcting himself, "he never sings them without consulting papa. Well, yes, this once more, as these ladies and gentlemen are so kind as to call for it."

Holding Lucy's hand, with his knee on the

sofa, and a steady serious look into the faces of all the company, he struck into "MULLIGAN'S WEDDIN'," in which his little clear pipe, trying to struggle conscientiously with the Irish patois and brogue, and his perfect and earnest seriousness, had the most curious effect:

> "Dere was feastin' and fightin',
> De neighbours delightin',
> And singin' and pratin'
> And *lots* of the batin'
> At Mulligan's weddin'.
> Whack foldi dididdle follero !
> Whack fol di di do !"

They were delighted with this little performance. The doctor enjoyed it. "A capital song, sir, and well sung. Thank you, sir."

The little man replied, with a bow, "I am so glad you liked it."

"I dare say, sir, you have plenty more on your list," said the doctor, "and would favour us."

"No, no," the Colonel interposed; "that will do very well. In fact, it is time to be thinking of bed. What do you say, little man?"

"Whatever you please, papa." Then to Lucy:

"Did you like 'Mulligan's Weddin'?'" Then he began to laugh with a hearty child's laugh. "So funny, you know—a wedding *here;* and then, Mulligan's. Ha! ha! Isn't it, now?"

"Getting late," said the doctor. "I must go and look after my stars. This will be a great night for observations. I shall search and search until I read something good there for Miss Lucy."

"And do you really do all this?" said the captain.

"I have a regular observatory, a fine glass, a meridian no less, and go regularly to work. Do you ever see the 'Southern Counties' Times'? No, I should say not," added the doctor, laughing; "the circulation is limited, and the matter very local. Well, there is an astronomical letter there every week from the present speaker."

"I should like to see it very much," said the captain; "I once had a little taste that way myself."

"Put on something warm and come," said the

doctor. "It's only across the lake, and my boatman is waiting."

The little man had been listening with distended eyes. He put up his mouth to Lucy: "Whisper," he said; "make them take *me*. Oh, *do!*"

The doctor heard him. "And why not?" he said. "We would not keep him long, and Captain Hallam could bring him back, though it *is* rather late."

The little man crowed with delight, and clapped his hands. "Let us go at once! Come!" And he began to pull at the doctor's arm.

The father, who was at the other end of the room, heard something of this, and came over. "At this hour? Not to be thought of, my dear child! Folly! I can't allow it. Go to bed."

Utter blankness and misery came into the boy's face, and he hung down his head.

"My dear child," said his father, lifting him till the child's face was on a level with his own, "why, you would catch cold in your chest, and take ill, and die; and then what would become of poor old papa? To-morrow we will drive over to this gentleman's."

The boy gave a deep sigh of disappointment, but of resignation. He looked back wistfully towards the doctor, who embodied such exquisite and ravishing charms—instruments that turned, and screwed, and went up and down; an inexhaustible source of entertainment. But he turned to his father.

"Papa, I should not like to take cold, and die, and leave you. So please to ring for Andy to come and take me to bed."

At that moment the door opened, and a short figure of a man, with a curious quaint head, stood looking in. He peered round, and then, without the least concern or consciousness of any one's presence, called out, with a nod,

"Master Ned, it's time now. Come, Sur!"

"Go," said his father. "There's Andy come for you. Wish all these ladies and gentlemen good night."

This ceremony the little man achieved with

courtly form, going round and putting out his hand, and in the ladies' instance, putting up his cheek for the kiss which he seemed to know would be inevitable. The father's turn came last, and he lifted him up to give him a warm embrace, and looked after him with rapt fondness. Taking Andy's hand, the little man walked away.

Then the clergyman and his wife and the rest took their leave for the night. The captain and the doctor came into the hall muffled in great-coats. It was a fine clear night, and they could see the stars without the aid of the doctor's telescope. The lake was at the back of the house, and the doctor's own boat was waiting—" My cab," he always called it.

But the Colonel and Mrs. Winter sat long in the drawing-room after all the rest had gone, talking, we may suppose, over some passages in life, long gone by. The French clock on the chimney-piece struck twelve, and half-past twelve, and one. Lucy had not yet gone to her bed-room, but fluttered nervously about the hall and passages and now ghostly dining-room. For she knew very well what troubled pictures were raised in the drawing-room. Suddenly the door opened, and he came out with a candle; as he saw her, he suddenly started back, but recovered in a moment.

"Oh!" he said, "how strange, how wonderfully strange! For the moment I thought—no matter now—you ought to be asleep, my dear child."

"I was waiting, dear Cousin Edward, to say good-night to you."

CHAPTER V.

THE EVE OF THE MARRIAGE.

THE next morning, the faithful Irish Andy came familiarly into the breakfast-room, with the most perfect composure, and told the company that "the masther" was not "himself at all," and that he, Andy, had thought it better to keep him in bed. He had now come for a "sup" of weak tea, and such-like. "Indeed," Andy went on, entering on a narrative, as he himself took up the teapot, "I don't know what's coming over him lately, the crature. I don't like the way he's in at all now; there's the truth, and no lie. His chist's always wrong—always, always—and I'm not pleased at all with the way he's in. And he'll see no docthors, and he has the old thing always on his mind."

They were a little alarmed at this description, which was indeed true; for as any one might have read from the Colonel's face, he was *always* ill, and at the moment of his arrival brought with him a heavy cold and cough which he did not care to tend or try to cure beyond the "little sup of tea," which Andy had brought up. Yet by the middle of the day he had forced himself, as he always did, to get up and go about, and said he was perfectly well.

That day was an almost feverish day. It was the day before the marriage, and a hundred things "turned up" and presented themselves after lying back expressly, as it were, and which had to be done, and done hurriedly.

Yet neither mother nor daughter was "put out" by this flutter, nor was there need to mark them "dangerous" as is common with too many persons on such occasions. The mother and daughter sat together and talked, sometimes of the great event that was drawing near, but in truth a good deal more of the guest who had arrived last night. He was gone out, and from the windows they had seen him holding his "little man's" hand as they both walked off together round the lake on the promised expedition to the doctor's observatory.

That day passed by too quickly. But towards evening all had been done that was to be done. They had been down to the church—a charming little village church—rather new, its tower and spire being tiled over with warm genial tiling, made out of the clay of the place. The genteel people of the place were for the best Welsh slates, but the vicar and his architect felt that there was fitness in this local covering. The village people had worked very hard and decorated the inside very prettily. The Colonel was nearly all the day away at the doctor's house, looking at the instruments, in which his boy found such a fascination. They came home towards four, and as they walked up the avenue, the boy's hand still in his, and he in a sort of reverie, they saw a chaise at the door with a portmanteau on it. This awakened him, and he stopped a moment. " More company," he was thinking; "this was not the place for me to come to."

In the hall he met Lucy in all her impetuosity and flutter. She started when she saw him.

"Come with me, Colonel Edward," she said, hastily taking his arm. "Won't you? I want to show you something."

"My dear child," said he, fondly, "do not ask me. I cannot go through more of this. Seeing new faces always makes me miserable. I am a wretched oddity, but you know——"

"It is not that, dear cousin," she said, in great excitement. "There's no new face. Come to my room. I want— Yes," she added, suddenly, "to show you all my stores. Come, do."

"But, Ned," he said, absently, "we must find Andy somewhere. Where is he?"

Andy was found, and the Colonel went with her. She was strangely excited, and as she showed all her presents, seemed to be doing this as an excuse for approaching some subject, talking very rapidly all the time. He looked and admired in a sort of abstracted way.

Colonel Edward seemed to be awaking gradually. "But what is this? and *I* have contributed nothing! Goodness, what a being I am! I think of nothing. I don't know how to do anything like other people. You must let me make up for all this stupidity. Tell me quickly what you would like."

"Mr. Benbow," she said, colouring, "how kind you are!"

"But you must tell me," he said, more earnestly; "I don't understand these things. I am quite helpless—a bracelet, a necklace—you must tell me, and fix on something."

In her eyes was twinkling a sense of some eager and secret plan.

"There is a present you *could* give me, dearest cousin, which would make me—and make us all *so* supremely happy; but I know that you could not give it to me, and that I have no right to ask it of you."

"What is it?" he asked, eagerly. "I am so

glad to hear this. Let it be as big as you like. Don't be afraid."

" If I thought you cared for me enough," she said, hanging down her head sadly. "But I have no right to expect that, and you would think me forward, and——"

"But what can you mean, my dear child !" he said, wondering, and with a troubled air. "You know that I like you, and it would make me, oh! so happy, to be allowed to make you happier even in that trifling way ; for since I have come into this house, I seem to have come into a kind of peace that I have not known before, for from your eyes the old light seems to come, and I seem to be in a presence that I have long missed. And *you* think I could refuse you, when I seem to hear that voice, and to see those features ?"

With an impetuous motion she put her arm in his, and, with glowing cheeks and flashing eye, began to pour out an eager whispering—a perfect tide. Before she had done, he had drawn himself away with a start—drawn himself further and further away. He set himself free, and covered his face with his hands.

"This is not right. Impossible! I did not expect this from you!"

"Forgive me, you make me wretched. But you asked me to name the present I liked—you know you did, and I told you you would be angry;" and she glided down before him on to her knees.

He had walked away a little, then turned hastily, and saw her kneeling before him. "Dear child, you know not what you ask me. How can I—how *dare* I do it? He hates me and hates my boy." He was growing more and more agitated every moment. "You do not know the whole. You cannot understand. *Anything* but that—no! no! no!"

She rose slowly, and turned away impetuously.

"This was to be a happy day for me," she said, tossing her head. "They all told me so. Where is your promise *now?* Do you suppose *I* care for presents, and bracelets, and such things? You have made me feel a mortification that no one else has done—no one else ! Every one else has been good to me."

She walked away flushed and indignant. He stood a moment irresolute, then in a faint voice called her.

" Lucy, come back. I did not mean to be unkind. But if you were to know how I have suffered--what I suffer. But it may have been all wrong, and I promise you now I will try in future to think less uncharitably of one who has so deeply injured—not *me*, but——"

" Ah !" said she, running to him. " But *that* is not enough—that is a very trifling marriage present for *me*. Try ? You must give me more than that. Should you see him or meet him, you will promise me to write—to speak—to forgive— to hear him—tell him that you have misjudged him a little—that he has done nothing to——"

" NEVER ! I can *never* do that," he said, passionately. Then, suddenly checking himself, " Well, if it pleases you, I do promise. It will not be for long, and there is folly in all this. Some day—if *he* writes—I may——"

"This is a promise," she said, panting with eagerness; "a solemn one, mind; for I shall be away, and you will not see me again for long, and I have nothing to trust to but your honour and promise."

"Then you have it."

"The first time you see him?"

"Yes."

In a second she had flown away from him, and with a cry of delight called out:

"Spencer! Spencer!"

Spencer Benbow came hurrying from some room, then stopped irresolutely. Under the lamps stood the Colonel half turned away, and as his brother drew near, with his hand half raised. In a moment the eager girl had seized that gentle hand in both hers, and drawn it softly towards another that was half extended.

"You promised, you know," she whispered. It was no use resisting, and the Colonel turned a look upon his brother, which the other understood in a moment.

It was all over—the enmity of years was gone.

"Poor Spencer," he said, "I have done him sad injustice. Will you say it to him again? You recollect what I said to you and to Lucy—that he hated me and my boy. It was a shocking slander. I thought so, but I had no reason to think so. I must atone for all this," he added, wearily. "Give my love and affection to the pretty bride, and tell her I am only nursing myself for the morning."

This scene, reposing as it seemed, basking as it were in a softened mellow light, was often to be looked back to; that gay drawing-room, full of beaming and happy faces. They had little games, that almost verged on romping, at least where the "little man" was concerned, who was screaming and crowing with delight, hiding behind cushions and sofas, and burying his little face in ladies' skirts. He told his day's adventures again and again, and spoke with rapture of those *wonderful* instruments, the screwing and mechanical arrangements of which had penetrated him with delight and admiration. He had never seen such a world of apparatus, and

the doctor this very night, taking him by the
shoulders, had sworn he should go over to-morrow and assist at certain unscrewings and oilings
which were to take place. He sang them various
songs, and, on a general demand, stood up in the
middle and again gave " Mulligan's Weddin',"
with entire approbation. It was noticed that,
whenever he mentioned the name of that Irish
bridegroom, his little eye wandered roguishly to
the captain, who affected to be overcome with
bashfulness at such public notice. Occasionally
he assumed a grave face of responsibility, and
stole away to have a private interview with his
papa, coming back with a little air of decent
solemnity, saying, " I do not like the way papa
is in." But he soon freshened up into gaiety
again, until eleven o'clock came, and with it
Andy's curious face appeared at the door, with
his unconcerned, " Now, Master Neddy, it's time
for you ; come along."

CHAPTER VI.

THE WEDDING.

HERE was now the morning of the wedding, as sunny a morning as "though it were bespoke, Glory be to God," to use Andy's remarkable blessing. How bright the day was, and how bright and gay looked the deep red and green of the little place. Inside there was flutter, but delightful flutter — kissing, smiles, tears, and kissing again.

The Colonel is down betimes, but every one notices his face, and sees at once that he should be in his room. There is a great change in his looks within these two days, but he said he was well. But Andy, who had a sort of festive air himself, was heard to say, "he hoped it would all be right *to-morrow next day*"—a misgiving which was to be realized presently. Yet, with a generous foresight, the Colonel had not lost time; and on the night before a messenger had been sent up to Town, with a letter to the chief jeweller, and who returned betimes with a superb casket. As Lucy came to him, about eleven, in her bridal dress, all lace and white silk and white flowers, he put this into her hand. "This," he said, "is but a poor token of what I feel to you, and for what you did last night. It is a miserable present, but I have no time, and no judgment."

"It is superb," said she, taking out the jewels, which were magnificent, "and I am so happy !"

Captain Hallam was come for her. The carriages were waiting.

The little church was charming. The flowers seemed to have bloomed from the night before. They clustered over the pillars. The villagers filled the aisles. The young girls looked wistfully on, thinking, as every young girl does, of another picture where *they* would be the chief figure. Of all the pageants in life's many pageants and shows, this, perhaps, is the most interesting. The greatest churl among the spectators feels that this is not a mere scene in a play. Long after, when the last act has nearly begun, the performer looks back to that morning, and sees herself through a soft cloud on that morning, and thinks herself another being. Oh, how young! how pretty! how fresh! And how bright and fairy-like every-thing all round. It seems only as far off as last year, and she turns (by instinct) to look into that glass over the chimney-piece!

Mr. Winter was the celebrant of the office, and was " assisted " by a good-humoured clergy-man, the Rev. John Hallam, brother, as we may suppose, to the captain. The friends drew in close as the clergymen began their combined labours. Even at that moment the quick eyes of Lucy, darting about, saw that the Colonel was not there, though the little bright face of his son was to be seen, studying, with an absorbing interest, some mechanical arrangements on the stair of the pulpit. Andy, too, could be seen

afar off, towards " lookin' in " at the business
with a dry, serious, and inquiring look.   He had
just " run down from the masther."

It was done now.   The combined efforts of
the two clergymen had succeeded, and Lucy and
her lover, *Captain and Mrs. Hallam*, were walking away in a sort of reverential bearing.   There
was signing in the vestry, congratulations, kisses
so fervent, whispered " darlings ! "   " my pets ! "
Then a coming out and taking off hats, and
driving away.   Then there was the house again,
Arbour Hill ; and Lucy, bounding from the
carriage, fluttered straight to the Colonel's room.

He was on the sofa, and languid and pale.
After he had wished her all blessings and happiness, " My dear child, my dear *Lucy Hallam* "—
he said this very tenderly—" when it came to
the last moment, then I found I had not
strength, though I tried very hard.   My little
man will be here, I suppose, presently."

Then they all came home with a sort of
dropping fire.   Our doctor, who had hoped to
be there, was kept away by professional duty,

which came most awkwardly. Then the break-fast set in.

That, too, was of a very cheerful and festive pattern. Such things in the country have a tone of their own quite unique. That, too, is a picture to be looked back on in those coming days when we shall be looking into the drawing-room mirror, waiting for our married son and his children to come to dinner on, say, a Christmas. The affectionate voices, the fervent wishes, the *genuine* speeches, so different from other speeches over wine—these come back like the chime of the Christmas bells we have heard overnight.

There was a health or two, and a speech, kindly but hurried; for time was pressing, and a train was to be watched for. Spencer Benbow did this duty in a pleasant buoyant fashion, which kept away the faint clouds of gloom that were seen gathering. He told grandly of the bride's virtues, of the love they all bore to her, of her smile that lit up that house and delighted all who came within its charm—her cheerful spirit, which made all happy. There was the loss—but there was gain for another, who had secured a prize. Then there was another, who was not with them at *that* moment, but whose heart was with them, and who had tried to be of their company. He knew him; and never so well, as within a day or two, knew what were his virtues and his affection. However, it was not too late then.

During this speech the servants had gathered at the door, and were listening. Round the table were handkerchiefs very busy. The " little man" had listened with an air of deep attention, " taking it all in : " he was very happy, too, and had been supplied with wedding-cake under tolerably small restraint. Yet he was a little gentleman, and had trained himself not to indulge in excesses which he found but too common among his contemporaries. When Spencer had finished speaking of the Colonel, the little man softly stole from the room—not, as some unfairly suspected, because of the richness of the cake, but to pay a visit to his father. In a very few moments he came back, with a strange look of mystery and importance on his little face, got beside Lucy and her husband, and whispered eagerly :

"Papa is so much obliged for your kind reception of his name—those were his words—and wishes he was here himself to thank you all."

"Why not tell these ladies and gentlemen, my boy ?" said the captain. "Would you be afraid ?"

"Afraid ! why, papa gave the message."

In a moment there was a silence, and with his face modestly bent upon the tablecloth, the little man repeated the same words, and gave them his papa's message.

"Papa is so much obliged for your kind reception of his name—those were his words—and wishes he was here himself to thank you all."

"Ah, listen to the darling !" was said among the maids at the door ; "listen to him now."

"Shure he's wiser," said Andy, almost contemptuously at *their* surprise, "than a grown Christian!"

But the hour had now come. There was a general rising up—a rushing away for some last preparation—and more tears and embracing. The carriage was there, and they were all out on the steps. There is the last embracing and last good wishes; and Lucy, in sober travelling dress, yet magnificent, stoops down and lifts her veil to kiss the little man, who has put up his face. Now they drive away, and the "old shoe," searched for and found with difficulty, flies into the air after them. A cluster of faces, half sorrowful, half pleased, looked long after them.

Then came the lull—the sudden prostration which sets in after all such excitement. That day becomes of a sudden purposeless—a day for weary and vacant wandering, when no one can settle himself to anything. It was felt, too, that the light of that house had gone out, and that there was a change.

The Colonel, however, was not mending, and

they were beginning to be in serious concern about his state. And about four o'clock his brother said he would go over to the doctor's house, not two miles away round by the lake, and see if he had returned. The doctor knew of some greater doctor whom he had to meet not far away that very day, and who might be readily secured also. It was determined not to say a word of this little plot to the patient, who would raise difficulties, and protest he was getting well.

The little man soon heard of this proposal, and saw in it at once a plan for advancing his own little interest and pleasure.

"Oh, then, I can go too," he said, "and see all the telescopes again. I was *promised*, you know."

"The very thing," said Spencer; "we shall make an expedition together. But mind, now, not a word to papa. We are going for a great doctor, and if he hears it he will not see one, and perhaps he will never get well."

"Never get well," repeated the little man, anxiously.

"I mean," said the other, "if he does not see the doctor. None of us *can* be well unless we see doctors."

He had still some misgivings. "But," said he, wisely, "it is all for papa's good; and I *am dying* to see those telescopes again. Whisper; I'll not tell papa a word."

Andy appeared suddenly. "Where are you taking him to, Misther Spencer? Have you spoke with the masther about it?"

"Oh, all right, Andy, and quite right of you. But I'll make it all square. We are going for a doctor, and not a word is to be said to *him*, you understand."

Andy shook his head.

"Masther Neddy, you'd better go in and tell the masther *yourself*. That's the raysonable way."

"Now, Andy," said the young man, seriously, "you mustn't interfere here; we want to get a doctor. You don't understand these things. And you know very well how hard it is to get my brother to take care of himself."

" Oh, so be it; so be it," said Andy, coolly. " Only," he added, muttering, " wait until to-morrow next day."

" So we can, Andy, and till the day after too," said the young man, laughing.

The little man laughed too. " Oh, Andy," he said, " how funny. But *I think*, Andy, you don't *quite* understand."

The young man went to his room to get a coat and write a letter for the post. The little man was wrapped up in his coat, and ready for the road in a moment. He waited a little impatiently in the hall a few moments, and then went out through the garden round by the back of the house. Spencer Benbow had a longer letter to write than he fancied, and took a longer time over it, and then came out hastily. He found the little fellow gone.

" The impatient little rascal," he said. " He is busy with some tricks in the garden." But he was not in the garden. Then he hurried across the field, and was greatly relieved by hearing the voice of the little man calling to him cheerfully in a sort of chirrup of delight. He was playing "hide and go seek;" was up in a tree.

By one of those curious coincidences which are almost unaccountable, the Colonel, almost as soon as they had gone, thought of his little son, and rang his bell for Andy. The little secret about the doctor was now sure to come out.

"Sorra o' me knows where he is, Colonel. He said he was to go with the brother over to the docthor man."

"Gone with Spencer!" repeated the Colonel, starting up suddenly. "How dare you trust him out of your sight? Did I not depend on you?"

"Sorra a one o' me could help it," said Andy. "Sure I thought Misther Spencer was *now* next to yourself."

"To be sure, to be sure," said his master, colouring and letting himself fall back on the sofa. "You did quite right, Andy. The poor child can't be shut up altogether. But when will they be back, Andy?"

"Oh, be raysonable yourself now," said the other, coolly; "you know they are only gone now."

"Oh, to be sure. But mind, Andy, the moment they come in send him to me."

Meanwhile Spencer had gone hastily towards the lake, from whence the voice seemed to come.

"What folly of me," he said, "to let him go. Troublesome child!"

In a moment he caught sight of the "troublesome child," standing in a little punt which was drawn up close to the shore. He was in a tumult of delight, and clapping his hands eagerly, from sheer spirits.

"I found this," he cried. "Only think! We must go in this; it will be much shorter."

The bank overhung the river, and was very steep.

"Take care; do take care!" cried his uncle, in an agony of terror. "How did you get there? Stay where you are till I come down."

"But we must go in the boat, mustn't we?" said the little fellow, standing in the bows with one of the small oars in his hands. " We will bring the doctor over in it to papa, and lose no time."

" What folly of me ! " said Spencer to himself, hurrying down the little side-path which wound down to the water. The water was concealed from it by some furze-bushes. He long after recollected that picture of the fine little fellow standing at the bow of the boat, flourishing the light oar. Long after, also, he recollected the wild start he got when he reached the edge and saw that the boat seemed to be *empty*, and was moving slowly away from the shore. He could not reach it; he was quite helpless, and the little boy had not strength to manage it.

" He must be hiding at the bottom of the boat ! " he said, for so he thought he was.

He called out to him frantically, " Come back. Give up nonsense, pray, dear child, for your father's sake. We shall not be able to get the boat back without all sorts of trouble."

He paused, but there was no answer.

He called again. The boat was gliding

further away; and then a sudden chill struck to his heart. He was near fainting with the bare idea. He climbed up the bank, not by the path, struggling up with his hands and feet, and then he saw that the boat was empty, with a solemn emptiness that made his heart shrink. The sight of his eyes seemed to leave him. Down below him the water was black, and dark, and deep, and weedy; and though he could not swim, his impulse was to fling himself down, cast himself in at all risks, and, if he could not save, hide himself from the world for ever. But a happier glimpse of reason came to him, and gasping, and staggering, he climbed up the bank yet higher on to the road, and shouting, made for the house.

There was now a figure actually coming down towards him, sent, as it seemed, by Heaven. "Oh, Andy, Andy!" he shrieked. He could do no more, and pointed back. The faithful retainer understood enough (he had been "rared" on the Donegal coast). He was past Spencer in a second, and in another was at the water's-edge.   A little cap was floating there, and told him the story and the spot.   The boat was drifting far out, and seemed a figure of all chance and hope drifting away also.   With a " Holy Mother ! " on his lips, Andy had gone in head-foremost among the weeds.   He had once made one in a life-boat crew on that Donegal coast.   He was sure to succeed in what he had tried, and he dived, and searched, and explored, and at last came upon the little helpless figure, bound up tightly in a mass of cruel weeds.   Andy had now hard work to set him free.   But he did so at last.   But one so young and tender as the child was, and now so many minutes under the water—there he was now, on the bank, limp, saturated, and his soft hair covering his face ; and as for life——

Andy had him in his arms in a moment.

Not knowing what he was doing, Spencer put out his hands to help ; but Andy shook him off with a fierce " Stand back ! "

" What shall I do ? " said the other, wildly.

" Will he live ? Have I killed him ? Tell me. Tell me something to do."

Andy was struggling up the bank with super-natural strength.

" There, run, run round for the doctor for the bare life, if you do care for *his* life at all."

In the kitchen, before the great fire, was a strange and terrified group round their insensible figure. No one knew what to do—hot water and hot things were the only resource until the doctor, whom God sent quickly, should arrive. But up-stairs the quick ear of the father had heard the rustling and rushing, and the half cry and half whisper. A yet quicker instinct made him associate this disorder with something connected with his child. Weak as he was, he had risen and come out into the hall. He heard the quick voices—the confusion below— and rather staggered than walked to the top of the stairs. At the same moment, he met Mrs. Winter ; her pale face and despair told him everything.

"Where is he?" he said, in a trembling voice. "What is all this?"

"Oh, come, come!" said she, bursting into tears. "You must prepare yourself—the poor, poor darling—the boat——"

He could not answer her, but stood looking at her with a fixed stony air, swaying from side to side as if about to fall.

"No, no; you must not—not that way!" And she caught him in her arms, and tried to stop him. But he put her aside, almost roughly, and went down.

The wretched brother was the first that met him, who shrunk away as though he wished the earth to cover him. Then the miserable father put aside the group that was humanely striving to hide what was lying there from him, and fell forward on the floor beside the helpless body of his "little man."

But the faithful Andy had great "sinse," as he called it, and good practical skill for the common emergencies on that Donegal coast. "Many and many's the time" a poor fisherman had been carried ashore in that poor way, and they had got him round. And here now, as he was working himself, and making them all work, rubbing, fomenting, and warming, the sounds of wheels came most gratefully to their ears, and made Andy break out into a hearty " Glory be to God for all his mercies ! " In another moment a doctor was stamping down the stairs, swiftly as if on life or death ; and " Glory be to God," as Andy would again say, another doctor was following. What they had come for, though, there was no one up-stairs to tell them, and no messenger could have reached them.

But the unhappy father, removed from that place up-stairs, had come to himself. His grief had taken a new shape — of vengeance. " I knew it ! God's justice may overtake him. The villain plotted it. God punish him for it ! He came here for it. And you brought us to this wretched house for the same thing. But I shall live to be revenged. I told you so. The vile black villain ! He murdered my poor wife, and now comes to destroy my poor, poor child. Let him come and kill me—-now—no, but he sha'n't ; I shall live, live to destroy him, if only for that.   Where is he ? where is he ?   Let me find him !"

CHAPTER VII.

THE FALL OF SPENCER BENBOW.

One of the characters in this little rural
piece was that worthy Doctor Legge, who had
now arrived, a curious compound of jollity
and mechanical science. He was ingenious in
manufacturing telescopes and other astronomical
instruments, the discoveries which these enabled
him to make he was fond of exhibiting to his
young friends. He declared he was for "spying
out the nakedness of the land." Notwithstanding
his "observations," and his jollity, the practice
of the pleasant doctor did not sensibly increase.
He had a family to maintain, and on the shutting
up of the "big house," after Mr. Benbow's death,
had seriously thought of emigrating or going
away to New Zealand. When he was offered

the post of surgeon to one of the vast ocean steamers, he accepted it with eagerness and alacrity, on the ground that "it would give him time to look about him."

The day of his departure was at hand, and indeed he only waited for the wedding. His present, on this auspicious occasion to the bride, was a handsome opera-glass.

When it became known in the parish that the doctor was leaving, there was much concern. But, as he pleaded, "a man can't support a family on surgical and optical instruments exclusively." He thought himself lucky enough to be able to remain for Lucy's wedding, though, as he said, he was running it far too close for comfort or safety, and that evening was to set off by the evening express. His farewell to his family was warm and touching ; but our doctor said he would soon be home again, and with them all in ten months. On this night of departure, as there was an hour to spare, he went up to his "observatory," so he called it, to have a farewell look at his instruments, and get his large telescope

into position for " one last look." He seemed
to take farewell of them as he would of his dogs
and other favourites. He busied himself putting
away these precious objects carefully, for fear the
children should damage them.

While he was thus engaged there entered to him
of a sudden Mr. Gordon, who was still in office.

" This is a day of festivity," he said bitterly.
" What jollity and merry-making !' Yet they
did not think fit to ask me. But my enemy
was there."

" My dear friend," said the other, " I haven't
a moment to speak to you—only half-an-hour to
catch this train, so don't interrupt me."

" Happy man," said the other, " going to seek
your fortune."

" Pretty fortune," said the other impatiently;
"a ship's surgeon; but don't talk to me now.
Amuse yourself; look through that telescope;
only don't worry me now."

The other did as he was bidden to do. And
in a mechanical sort of way put his eye to the
telescope.

"Ah," he said, "the old place. There it lies —where I spent so many happy hours. There are the gardens—how neglected they are now! I dare not enter there—they would turn me out like any tramp."

"Cheer up, old man," said the doctor, still bustling about; "there are good days in store for you yet."

"And there is the lake—on which I used to row so carelessly, when I thought there were no real cares in life. What a change for me!"

"Well, you have your nice wife—and your pretty little girl, and——"

"Good gracious!" he cried, "why there's that boy!"

"What boy?" said the doctor.

"Yes! he's getting into the punt, and by himself. He'll be upset! What folly!"

"You don't mean to tell me the Colonel's little fellow? They ought to look after him better than that."

"Ah, there's some one coming down now."

"Ah! I knew they'd look after him," said the

doctor, impatiently. "Why, it's Edward, the brother—he's calling him back from the bank, and waving his hands. And now he's running down through the trees to the edge. Good heavens! the child's tumbled over the side—he'll be drowned. Help! help!"

The doctor called to his companion, as if both were close to the scene. Such was the deception produced by looking through so powerful a glass.

"Oh, I forgot," he said in despair, "we are a mile and more away. We can do nothing."

"Wait! wait!" said the other, who had now his eye to the glass, "some one has now plunged in—and he's got hold of the boy. There! he's safe."

"You don't say so," said the doctor, eagerly, and turning back from the door which he had reached. "Well, this is exciting!"

"And he's swimming with him—and—he's got to the shore now—and the other is helping him out."

"Who's helping him out?"

Gordon turned away, and in a low voice said, " Why, that Spencer ! "

" I'll be wanted badly now," said the doctor. " I'd better run up as fast as I can ! Oh, but I forgot ! I can't lose the train—as my ship—never mind, you'll run as fast as ever you can, and fetch my deputy—now mind—don't lose a second, for time's vital. Now to say good-bye to all below." And the good doctor, who was before all a man of business, dismissed sentiment as a thing he was not concerned with at that crisis, and after his adieus rushed off to catch the night express, which he accordingly did.

Nothing would do. Everything was tried. The faithful Andy even put his lips to the luckless child's, and by inhalations tried his best to restore him. But gradually, after a faint flicker, life flickered out, and the luckless Colonel stood there bereft of his treasure and his darling.

" *Where, then, is that murderer ?* " were his first words. " Let me see him."

His brother, blanched with terror and grief, had in vain been telling to others all that had·

occurred. The boy had escaped from him, had got into the boat of himself, and despairing of him he had shouted; plenty of people must have heard him. He had gone to his rescue.

There was a curious air of incredulity. It was very awkward, and facts appeared strongly against him. His brother in all his despair found composure enough to denounce him thus publicly.

"Look at him! There he stands!" he said; "the murderer of my child. Was it not his interest? Who threatened me when he found that I had been left my own lawful inherit-ance? Whose interest was it? Before Heaven I say there stands one that did it—THE MURDERER."

Standing among those to whom this was addressed—and he had come up in the hurry of excitement—was Mr. Gordon. To him the unfortunate younger brother appealed in his despair.

"You know me well; you do not think I could do this; say one word,—clear me!"

The other paused, and then turned away silently.

The results of that catastrophe were most serious for all concerned. Colonel Edward went out on the world, crushed out of all life and hope. For Spencer — no pariah could have envied his condition. The denunciations of his brother had been taken up by the whole district and repeated. He was met with averted eyes, and with scorn shunned; no one addressed him word or letter. Then, after a time, general indignation broke out loudly. The matter should be taken up publicly, and an official investigation follow. It was intolerable. As well might an infected person be allowed to go about with impunity.

Spencer Benbow's bearing under this treatment was calm and courageous, and, as they considered it, " worthy of a better cause." But it was only defiance at best—the insolence of guilt. He calmly told his story to the few that would listen; and many recalled the memorable day when the grand jury and magistrates being assembled for the assizes, a leading county gentleman made a speech to his brethren, and said he thought it exceedingly bad taste and questionable policy, in one who lay under so grave a suspicion, to associate with the gentlemen of the place; he should at least wait until he had cleared his character. He would beg of him to retire, and not come among them any more. The face of Mr. Benbow grew pale. In a low tone he could only protest his innocence. He had no evidence; how could he find it? He made a fervid and almost earnest appeal to them against the treatment which he had received, and was receiving. Nothing, however, would do. He was pressed to go away, as nothing he could do would restore him.

During the course of this treatment a strange change seemed to be wrought in him. The iron, in his phrase, had eaten into his soul. The struggle against the injustice, as he conceived it, was leaving many a line upon his face; where could be traced a bitter hostility. All his old openness and cheerfulness seemed to give place to a cold, hard, and even desperate manner. It was indeed no wonder. He was a ruined man for life; no one can fight successfully against public judgment once it has condemned. What were Benbow Towers and all his estates to him? The awful rumour pursued wherever he went. First came the looks askant of those with whom he worked in London; then the awful summons to the parlour where his chiefs sat in council.

"We cannot avail ourselves of your services any longer, Mr. Benbow," said they; "indeed, were we inclined to do so it were impossible, for your companions refuse to work with you. These rumours may be untrue, and we devoutly trust you will one day clear yourself, but under the circumstances it is undesirable you should remain."

Thus was he *chassè*!

The same fate pursued him everywhere. The dreadful story was in the papers, and furnished a subject for a novel. There was no hope for him and no outlet, unless indeed he would change his name, as he was advised, and go and hide in America.

This he disdained to do. He would wait for his vindication—one day it might come.

No one would associate with him now. This treatment, however valiant and courageous might be his resistance, he was powerless to resist; and crushed by the neglect and open dislike of the district and shunned like some pariah, he quitted the place. He could never enjoy them. His story — duly magnified — followed him wherever he went, and there was clearly nothing left for him but to hide his head in a foreign country.

This was a terrible thing for one so ambitious and one just starting in life, full of hopes and aspirations. He had tried every resource to extricate himself, but there was no hope of that. There were no resources that ingenuity could supply, so he saw that he must only submit or wait.

CHAPTER VIII.

REHABILITATED.

A YEAR had passed away since the death of the little boy, where there was great joy caused by the sudden return home of the excellent doctor after his voyage. The annual Dipchester Ball was being given on the night he arrived; and the doctor, always ready for anything where fun or spirit was concerned, set off at once, to show himself to his friends and pick up all the news, "from where he left off," as he said.

It was at the supper-table, when after all the greetings were over he gaily questioned his friends.

"Benbow gone away, and under a cloud; and why?"

There were significant looks and headshakings,

and it was not for some moments that the reason was explained to him.   He started.

"Good heavens!" he exclaimed.   "Don't you know? He wasn't near the boy. Why, I saw it all. I know all about it; and there's Gordon. he saw it too, and knows all about it!"

A large group had now gathered round him, in utter astonishment, and eager to listen.   He went on: expressions of astonishment broke out!

"We were looking through the telescope, and I was standing beside him packing as hard as I could. I was as close to the whole business as if it was going on in the street below there, or under the window. The figures and faces were as clear and bright as yours there. But where's Gordon? Ask him. Send for him; he saw the most."

The doctor was a shrewd, sensible man—and saw the necessity of acting with caution.

"Don't let this get about," he said suddenly. "Good heavens! what cruel injustice! But we must clear Benbow in the fullest and most satisfactory way. I must see him first. It's quite clear. It's revenge for something."

In a week's time the assizes were to be held at Dipchester. There was " a heavy calendar," and an unusual attendance of country gentlemen. When they were assembled in the grand jury room, rumour reached them that Mr. Benbow was in the town, and was coming up to see them. There was indignation loudly expressed at this. But the doctor interposing, bid them wait, and they would hear something that would surprise them. He then withdrew and presently entered. Everybody was expectant. Suddenly entered Mr. Benbow. He was stern and resolute.

" My brother is dead," he said. " The news reached me a few days since."

This was an unexpected piece of news. Still it was strange and rather undignified in the heir to present himself in this hasty, eager way.

" I know," he went on in the same tone, " I know your opinion of me. You think I am all but a murderer—or that but a faint line separates what I have done, or am supposed to have done, from murder. You also hold this view, I presume?" he added, abruptly turning to Gordon.

The other turned away his eyes in a guilty fashion.

"What! you hesitate?" said Benbow, suddenly, and with less of his old severity; "then say out plainly that you do *believe* me innocent, that you *knew* me innocent—me, your old friend. Come!"

There was something so earnest, so pleading in this appeal that it struck all with a strange sense as of something dramatic being at hand. They waited; Mr. Gordon faltered, looked at Mr. Benbow, then round at the rows of expectant faces. What could he do? How could he retreat without disgrace? He said:

"No, no; I must think with the rest—at least I know nothing to make me——"

"Know nothing!" said Mr. Benbow, in a loud voice. "Sure?—certain?" He paused. "Then is Dr. Legge here?"

The doctor entered suddenly. It may be conceived what a scene followed this apparition.

The doctor told his story. The wretched man fell on his knees, and made an agitated confession. Nothing could be more clear or convincing, and from that instant Mr. Benbow was restored to his old good repute.

A few weeks later, Spencer Benbow was known to have returned to his castle. It was noted that his hair had whitened. That was a remarkable scene when the gentlemen of the district — grand jurors, &c.—assembled at the Town-hall and declared their deep regret that any reports should have gone about affecting the character of Mr. Benbow; and declaring that they had the completest confidence in his honour. He was invited to receive an address to this effect, and be restored to his position; and he did accordingly repair to the room in which they were assembled. But they hardly reckoned on the reception which this well-meant *amende* was to receive.

"This," he said, "I suppose, is your atonement to me for your cruel injustice; for your destruction of me and of my house by these slanders! You are sorry for it, are you? Can you repair the wrong?—mend what has been broken? I can do all that myself. I ask nothing from you—neither your sympathies, nor your apologies, nor your regrets. I warned you, recollect, that you were destroying me; but you did not heed. You would not know me any longer, you said. *What if I do not know you?*"

These burning words, taken down in short-hand by eager reporters, invited specially to record something agreeable, were spread over the county, and, it must be said, were generally considered spirited and well deserved. No one was more completely rehabilitated. Mr. Benbow acted in the future as he had spoken, and very truly cut the county people. " I banish you," he seemed to say with Coriolanus, " from that hour." The county had the disagreeable duty of looking on while Mr. Benbow slowly built up the fortunes of his house. The people of the place were not his people. They saw others come in their place, invited from great houses. Every-thing he touched seemed to prosper. He had hosts of wealthy and titled friends to supply the place of those who had rejected him—and whom he rejected now.

One, and one only, was exempted from this contemptuous indifference—viz. the man whose silence had all but proved his ruin—and from that hour a sort of blight seemed to have fallen on him. Mr. Benbow spoke to him plainly.

"Your act was diabolical and malignant, for I've never injured you. I might as well compromise a felony as pass it by. Punishment must, and shall, overtake you. You know not what I suffered during those wretched months—so prepare. Vengeance shall come upon you and a terrible chastisement." His voice trembled as he spoke to him. "Go: you know you cannot remain here. The office you enjoyed so long is taken from you. But that is not all. *I shall hunt you down.* Wherever you go, this story shall go with you."

"I have a family," he pleaded; "my poor girl —her mother—for their sakes be merciful."

"No," said the other. "At least you shall suffer some of the agonies you made me suffer."

Mr. Gordon, shunned, pointed at, and having lost all he had in the world, had to go out on the wide sea of the world, to seek the fortune which he was not to find. He was soon forgotten. Indeed in two or three years, when Mr. Benbow was travelling on the Continent with his new wife, this wretched, broken man, almost in rags, found his way back, and came to beg half-crowns from the doctor and other good friends. At last he found his way back to Dipchester, and then Mr. Benbow relented, and got him into an alms-house. There he soon died, having left, it was said, an only daughter, who had ran away long ago. While Mr. Benbow's history was borne in mind, and had all the attraction of a romance.

Soon it was heard that a high and important marriage had been contracted—important in wealth, rank, and connection. Mr. Benbow had married Lady Anne Durden, daughter of an important Earl. He had an only son, who was now a youth of nearly twenty. Spencer Benbow was a great personage indeed, but known as a cold, hard, pitiless being, bent on the one aim of advancing himself and his family. He was never known to do anything kind or gracious, though he gave charity abundantly after an official system.

And now, while all these events have been related, and we have been stretching back our gaze into the past, Mr. Benbow has still been in his pew—his mind, it may be, wandering away also—skimming lightly over those grave events that were so portentous for him. It was like the Eastern who put his head for an instant into the tub of water, and then saw backwards through a whole life. There was the little boy's tablet, seen so very often. But it was only at the close of the service, and as the organ was breaking out in jubilation, that he noticed a new bluish marble slab on the wall, low down, near the ground. It was strange he had never remarked it, and through his glasses he read the past name " JAMES GORDON." He started — forgot his august companions — and even as they defiled out hastily whispered the beadle, "Who put up that tombstone? Quick."

"A lady, sir, a daughter of the unfortunate Mr. Gordon."

Mr. Benbow muttered:

"It should not have been put in such a place."

Then he turned to his Duke, and attended him to his carriage.

END OF PROLOGUE.

CHAPTER I.

THE Benbow family, as we have seen, were settled close to Dipchester, and, as it were, kept that antique little town fresh and sweet. When their great coach trundled in state through the long street which was the spine of the place, or their more quiet brougham, which had the significant dignity of a nobleman in plain black evening dress, the general pulse was much stirred—it was like a king, or, rather, grand duke, visiting his subjects.

Yet they were merely a private family, and not very rich; but there was an idea that they had immense influence, through intricate connections, which branched out like veins in the human body, and the blood which all flowed from the great centre Benbow heart. Dukes, marquises, prime ministers, were supposed to consider any wish or any request of the head of the Benbow family with respect and acquiescence. There were lords—old, as well as some newly run from the heraldic mould—planted about the district; some more wealthy even; but they were felt not to have *power*, and Dipchester did not abase itself before them.

The town itself, to the antiquary, was charming and inviting: to the bagman, or to the soldier mind, only a poor sort of a place: geographically, very many miles behind the disagreeable district of " Godspeed." There was no railway, no amusement to speak of, and but little business: all these flourished at the greater manufacturing town, some eight or ten miles away. Its one street wound, like a snake, in pleasant bends, lined with low houses, some of them overhanging the path, and of the genuine framed pattern. The old Queen Anne's brick— close, smooth, firm, and bright—asserted itself everywhere with a bold independence, flourished

in an honest glowing health, like the cheeks
of a fresh country girl, and seemed to betoken
a fresh stirring circulation inside.

The old Town-hall, with a stone-bewigged
Royal George in front, its pediment beams of
a dark-varnished oak, mixed with the cheerful
red ground, seemed as gay and as well burnished
as a Dutch house. The old inn, "The Swan,"
was of the snug roadside pattern, with its
wooden banner hung outside. It had its parlour, with sloped sides, like a ship's cabin; its
snug bar, low rooms, and alarmingly funereal
beds, which nodded and trembled as the guest
clambered in, and made him think uncomfortably he was under a catafalque, and laid out
for the night.

But, in its own estimation, Dipchester was
raised to the dignity of a perfect metropolis
by one feature; though in other points, the
inhabitants were accustomed to think and speak
poorly of themselves, with a sort of sad depreciation, owning their unhappy geographical position,
" at the back of Godspeed," with a Heep-like

humility. This was the little theatre—or rather, the Theatre Royal, Dipchester—which in such a place, acrimonious in its religion and so contracted in size, was a phenomenon. It, indeed, owed its existence to an accident: in fact, to an hilarious and enthusiastic subscription by the gentlemen, years ago, who wished to "play" themselves, and who had run up the little temple. It was quaint enough in its way, standing in a little bye-quarter, looking into a patch of green common, and having "Theatre" more legibly written on its face, by its style and bearing, than it is on such places now. For it had a sort of jocund, irregular look about it, and its wood-covered roof; while up to each of its three doors arose a small ship-cabin staircase, with a little shed or porch over all three, which went up and down with the steps. There were strange smells haunting the place, defying control, most insubordinate on the grand nights —or, the one grand night—of the year. This dreadful enemy would rise slowly from the pit about the middle of the performance; but, with a gallant self-respect which deserved all praise, was privately endured with a smiling consciousness, and wholly ignored by the boxes. What kept the little house was the tradition that Mr. Kemble had performed there one night. He was passing by on his way to " a gentleman's seat "—so Mr. Haggerston, the lessee, would tell the story—and was waylaid by an old comedian and friend—then manager—Gubbins; and in a noble and gracious way consented to give " The Stranger."

" And talk of generosity, charity, and doing the handsome thing," said Mr. Haggerston, relating the incident in his box-office as a sort of bonus to the ticket-taker, " where will you find 'em, except in the Profession ? A man like that—that had kings and hemperors at his feet—that had but to say, ' Give me a hundred,' ' two hundred,' aye, ' five hundred pounds, and I'll play for you, but not till then '—to think of his coming in, like you or I, in a simple, unhorsetentatious way, with no more pride in him than the commonest supernoomery ! He stood, sir, where you are standing at this very moment, and held a conversation with Dumbleton, the previous box book-keeper!"

Pretty walks lead into Dipchester; and of a fine morning, whether going or coming, we meet along the high road the great waggon and its four horses, the cheerful tramps, and, most frequently, the travelling artists, who carry portions of a divided show, the husband half, the wife the rest—artists without a theatre, and thrown more upon their own resources than any other members of the profession.

Not very far away from the little town we arrive at the gate of Benbow Towers—the temple in which the great "Boss" of the district is enthroned, and where he enjoys his worship. This Spencer Benbow, Esq., was great among the little squirelings of the place; but the feeling was as of strange, untitled influence among the mysterious dukes and marquises before alluded to—this simple commoner, who seemed to be as great as they, and even more remarkable for his want of title; as the black coat of Castlereagh made him more *distingué* among the blaze of decorations about him. What a wonderful match that was which he contrived for his eldest daughter, nothing less than the Marquis of Kimbury's eldest son! For his second, he found Lord Robert Purfleet; but for his own and only son, Charles Benbow, it was known that he was planning, building, digging, burrowing, and lying awake hundreds of nights, to construct an alliance of the most splendid sort, to which end he had selected a political Duke's daughter — Lady Rosa Fulke, one of three—and which alliance would be the crowning of the edifice. All to this end, also, would Benbow Towers, at fitful intervals, change from a dignified and morose bearing — a kind of grand, Manfred-like solitariness—into a gay and splendid activity, glittering and sparkling with lights, and teeming with life.

This almost pantomimic change would take place in a night. It would be found, of a sudden, that the great mansion was full of noble company—seen dimly and afar off by the common herd. Sometimes it was a duke, sometimes a political chief, or great general, but always persons in whom power as well as rank were joined. A smooth, reverend man would be seen in the garden, in black felt wide-awake, gaily chatting with Miss Lydia Benbow —that was his Grace of Canterbury, come for change of air for a few weeks. A jovial, burly gentleman would turn into the avenue on one of Mr. Benbow's horses—that was the Right Hon. James Hoxter, Secretary for some "Affairs" or other, now exactly like a plain country squire, which he was. Haughty and insipid dames, beautiful girls, gallant youths, all seemed to come and pass through Benbow House, as if it were a *douane*, or customs, where all were to contribute dues to the glory and advancement of Pelham Benbow, Esq.

These gatherings, as I have said, took weeks of painful gestation, and, though they cost vast sums, had each some aim or end intended, which more than repaid. If there was expense, there was calculation and certainty of return for that

expense. The man's—or gentleman's—whole
life had been a series of such measured calcula-
tions. So had he begun, so had he planned his
own rise, his own marriage with the Lady Mary
(she had been Lady Mary Tozer); so had he got
into Parliament; so had he laboriously effected
those joinings or friendship with the great, which
he made as fast and firm as if diamond cement
had been used; so had he obtained Benbow
Towers; so had he " got on " his family not from
any affection, but from finding in them qualities
which were useful to him; so had he married
his daughters; and so was he now planning his
last grand scheme, the marriage of his. son
Charles with the political duke's daughter.

At this time, when the present little melo-
drama begins, Benbow Towers, like its servants,
was in a blaze of gala livery, and, full of
company, seemed to glitter in its windows and
gardens like a piece of· silver cloth. The Duke
and his desired daughter, Lady Rosa, were there,
with many celestial political magnates, all chosen
with the greatest nicety, the most delicate

anticipated care, the most tender laying of trains —the length of each fusee being calculated with a mathematical exactness, so that the motives and baits should be touched at the precise moment, and all should "go off" together.

The present house-filling was, as it were, the loading of a piece of artillery, which, at the proper time, was to be laid and discharged, with a certainty of hitting what it was aimed at. There we see him now, sitting in his study, a general in a campaign at head-quarters, or a Von Moltke in a cabinet, laying out on paper all the operations. The rest of the family were carrying out these plans, unconsciously, and the pleasant entertainments of a country house were going forward—most of them there thinking they were asked but for their own merits, and to enjoy themselves.

This was his portrait—at least, what could be seen of him, from his desk upwards, where he was swimming, as it were, on the surface of paper billows, and waves of pamphlets. A long, flat face, white and hard, which mental exercise had dried up and "taken down," much as training affects the body. His eyes were faint and washy, instead of bold, bright, glistening orbits ; his hair was a sort of spare yellow covering. He was thin, worn wiry, always exquisitely clean as to shaving, and which seemed done by machinery; and as smooth and level in all his surfaces and edges as though he had been neatly cast in a mould. He spoke with a quiet precision in his voice, but quite distinctly, though a little husky. A microscope could not detect a speck on his clothes—his rather spare frock coat and light grey trousers—which always seemed of the same age, and, as his valet found, never could be got to grow old.

All this planning as time went on, grew into his nature. He cared little for the plan after all : it was the planning that was so fascinating. Such was this Machiavel of Benbow, as seen planning his great cast for the duke's daughter. The House for himself, the Duke's daughter for his son !—these were the levers with which he would prize open a peerage for himself, another seat for his son, then a fresh step up the baronial ladder. In short, the perspective of advancement he looked down was endless.

There was time before him. He was not yet forty-five. He all but doubled his life by rising at six, and going to bed at twelve or one; thus having eighteen or nineteen hours in his day, where most other men had but twelve or fourteen. He had indomitable energy, tact, and a quiet but irresistible force in all his actions.

He has just got away from the Duke for a short time—that magnate having despatches to write—when a knock is heard at the door, and a fair, tall, open-looking youth of eighteen stands in the door. There is a girlish air about him, from the pink and delicate colour of his skin; and there is a faint straw-coloured moustache, like a bit of floss silk.

"I cannot speak to you now, Charles," said the father in his low, measured tones—it was as if he were reading from a book. "But why are you not with Lady Rosa?"

" We are going out to ride in a moment; but I came to tell you, father, that Haggerston has come up about his ' bespeak,' as he calls it. He says he has got a wonderful actress—"

" Pray don't detain me with these childish things. Is your mind ever going to rise to the serious business of life ? I cannot see the man ; give him a subscription."

" But, my dear father, Lady Rosa is quite eager about it ; she says she is dying to see a country town theatre. And Mr. Hoxter is talking to the Duke now about it."

Mr. Benbow laid down his pen.

" Oh, I must see about this at once, I fancy. Send Haggerston to me in a quarter of an hour. I shall speak to the Duke."

Mr. Haggerston, manager of the Theatre Royal, was a burly man, in a tail-coat, which, with his stoutness, gave him the look, as one of the gentlemen said, of a river buoy. His cheeks were flushed, and he had a cool, blunt, and familiar manner, that no doubt came from frequently addressing audiences. He was now in the library, with a party of gentlemen sitting round, and who were glad of something to amuse them ; for it had been snowing hard all the morning, and there could be no hunting. There was the Right Hon. Mr. Hoxter, chairman of the committee, as it were—-an impression to which the solemn oak and the almost parliamentary furniture of the room contributed. Other members present : Mr. Joseph Benbow, the host's cousin ; Colonel Hanly, "scion of a noble house ; " a young and clever barrister who wrote those smart and interesting letters in the ' Times' on clergy matters, signed " Loaves and Fishes," but whose real name was Addiscombe; Lord Alwyn Fox, and others.

" You have quite roused our curiosity, Mr. Haggerston," exclaimed the chairman. " Tell us some more about this wonderful paragon of yours. Effingham, you say ?—not a bad choice of a name to begin with."

" Mark my words, sir, when she gets to London, she'll draw the whole town. Before long, I know, we'll have the agents down here, trying her with ten and fifteen pound a week. I know that sort of game pretty well by this time. I saw her at a little twopenny-halfpenny theatre on the circuit, and *snapped* her up at once."

"Well, you did the same as the agents, you see, ha, ha!" said Lord Alwyn Fox.

"Who is she, do you know?" asked Colonel Hanly.

"I take her to *be*, gents," said Mr. Haggerston, speaking in a low, mysterious voice and looking round in a guilty manner, "something, 'ighly tip-top, as has slipped away from a noble family of the 'ristocracy, sir. She has an air—a presence —worth at the least five guineas and a half a week."

"And what piece have you chosen for us, Mr. Haggerston?"

"An evergreen!—a piece, sir, that will keep the boards as long as the taste for Billy Shake-spere reigns; there's a British pit to pay their money at the pigeon-holes. I allude to the 'Lady'—the 'Lady,' sir, of the immortal Lytton Bulwer, Bart."

" Ah, you mean 'The Lady of Lyons,'" said Lord Alwyn. "Dear sweet Pauline—what a lovable creature—so womanly. She was thrown away upon Claude, quite."

" A noble play, sir. Never knew it not to draw money. I suppose it is acted somewhere in the British dominions, every night. The sun never sets on that piece, sir."

Here entered Charles.

" My father wishes to see Mr. Haggerston in his study ;" and the manager hurried out.

He could not be free or familiar in *that* cold presence, but remained awkward and silent before the dry, cold potentate.

" I have consulted with his Grace, and the other gentlemen and ladies who are stopping here, and it seems they all desire to see whatever entertainment you have to offer. I must ask you to do the thing as handsomely as it can be done with your resources. Reserve a number of the very best places."

" I understand perfectly, Mr. Benbow, sir. Leave it all to me. I'll make it a kind of state visit, sir—pink and white calico, take down partitions between the boxes—"

"I beg—now really I *beg*," said his ruler, austerely, "there will be nothing so exaggerated or ridiculous.· Everything proper, but nothing beyond. No—er—gilt chairs or, anything of that kind. Now, do understand me, or .some one shall go down and see that these instructions are carried out."

"Depend upon me, Mr. Benbow. Everything shall be in the nicest taste—and my eternal gratitude, sir——"

"Thank you. Never mind that, for you owe me none. There, that will do, Mr. Haggerston."

CHAPTER II.

ENTER MR. GEORGE CONWAY.

ON the second day after the assembling of
the guests at the Benbows, when the distinguished forces were about forming in order of
battle for going down to dinner, there entered
two new arrivals. These were Lord Formanton
and his son Mr. Conway.

The coming of these personages had been
a matter of doubt; for the uncertainty was
almost in proportion to their importance, and a
look almost of happiness was to be noted on
the lined features of the host. For Lord
Formanton was a person in his eyes of exceed-
ing weight and influence, with connections in
the Ministry, and who had shown a particular
liking for Mr. Benbow; while his son and heir

was one of those promising finished young men, of whom great things are prophesied, and for whom everything in the world was to run smoothly. The good fairy who looked after him had indeed provided him—as such guardians do their favoured wards—with all her treasures of good health, good looks, good tastes, good accomplishments and manners. There are many young men of greater fortune and higher positions, from whom society expects but little; while there are a few less favoured, whom society follows with interest, having settled that they shall rise in the world and do pleasant things. This may be for some sympathetic attractions, felt even by those who do not see or come in contact with the person in question. In short, he is interesting.

Lord Formanton, the father of Mr. Conway the interesting, was a nobleman of great wealth, a busy lord, with a fine park and estate—a noble seat, Formanton. The rental was large, and that curious, incomprehensible heir, whom mammas could not make out, had been asked to this house and that, importuned to this castle and that; if he had made a point of it he might have had files of young ladies of good birth and condition drawn up for his inspection; a lane of rank and beauty down which he might walk and choose. But nothing could be made of the creature, though with unwearied perseverance they tried him with everything. He gave them credit for cleverness, owning that with a surprising instinct they *had* divined some of his tastes. Nothing could be made of him. He went about in an undecided fashion, half dissatisfied, half seeking for that philosopher's stone of the ideal soul above all the dross and imperfection of this world, which, if really found, would, by the fatal blight of familiarity and restlessness, in a short time be found unsatisfactory.

In every circle is to be found this being, who indeed, as it were, drives "a good trade" in the business, the good-looking "misunderstood one," who meets now and again one that can understand him a little, who is always in the end turning out a deception. Thus he has to pass on to another. In his early stages such a young man was Mr. Conway, but he gradually worked himself free of such affectation, though it took a long, long time. When urged to go into politics, the same nicety and hesitation pursued him. No party was up to his ideal: "the representation of a vast number of fellow-creatures seemed an *awful trust*, from which a man might shrink." At least he must try and fit himself for the solemn duty; and so the time, and worse, the opportunity, passed by. Thus with the many advantageous alliances that were proposed to him. That, too, was an awful trust, alas! not to be laid down, as could be the parliamentary one. But what distinguished him from others, and saved him from the category of "fop," "ridiculous stuck-up fellow," was, that all this was conscientious and genuine. It would have worn off like bad plating but for a calamity that really was to colour his whole life.

The present Lord Formanton was twice

married, as will be seen by turning to the Golden Book. His first wife, Mr. Conway's mother, was one of the most charming of women : sweet and amiable, charitable and good, as it were savouring the whole household with a delicate fragrance of simplicity, which is known and but to be described as "goodness." She was very young when married, and when Mr. George Conway was a youth, really looked like his sister. Her husband, a good-natured, rather foolish little peer, always fussy, but credulous, was busy with a hundred little trifles in the day, which, through the magnifier of a dull simplicity which never left his eye a moment, were enlarged to vast proportions.

They made a very happy trio. There was a softness and sweetness about her which was her special charm. The young worldling, her son, became natural, soft, gentle, and loving, when with her. Being with her, he thought education, teaching, and reading were all in her gentle face. She cared as much for him.

Conway had a friend a good deal older than

himself, for whom he had a sort of romantic admiration, and with whom he exchanged a good deal of his epicureanism and scepticism, and whom he would force his friends to admire rapturously. "I know no type of chivalry like him," he would say; "he is the noblest, most unselfish fellow in the world: gentle as a woman, brave as a lion. *He* was the first who *really said*, 'Go, poor fly,' which that snivelling Sterne only imagined his Toby saying." This person was a tall, slightly stooped man, a little grizzled, with a soft voice and eye. His gentle mother, Mr. Conway insisted, should appreciate and admire this hero, and she would have obliged him in a far more difficult thing than that. But why dwell on that marvel of stupid blindness, when all the town was looking on and smiling, and shaking its head? It duly prophesied, and saw its prophecy fulfilled. Lord Formanton and his son had gone away for a short voyage in a yacht which the most chivalrous of men had insisted upon lending; and Rochester had been conjured and implored, as he was a chivalrous man, to look after the dear mother whom they were to leave behind for a week only. The type of chivalry wrung his friend's hand, and with a certain reluctance, as though he were making a sacrifice, promised solemnly to do what was asked. Then came the nine days' wonder, the inquiries, the mystery, the telegraphing, and the "I saw it all along." When husband and son came rushing home, they found their house empty, their hearth desolate. The death of the erring wife soon followed.

In Mr. George Conway this blow caused a surprising change. He could not at first believe it. It was more likely that words had failed of their meaning, and men gone mad. Nature, life, religion, must have turned upside-down, if such a terrible belying of fair promise and innocence was allowed. When the truth at last came home to him, it quite changed him, and he had done with chivalry for ever. Further, though he scorned revenge, he secretly longed for an opportunity when he could strike some blow, take some step which should commit him, as it were, and show himself at least how he despised his former chivalry. In his manner and behaviour there was little changed: he affected to be all politeness and graciousness, but he was in a wary ambuscade, ready to welcome the first opportunity. That done, he felt that his soul would be more at rest. It was in this temper that he found himself at the Benbows, and in the humour also, that if he found any girl likely to fancy him he would enjoy tempting her to give him her heart, and would then depart with as little mark on his own as his yacht would leave on the waters behind her.

The peer was crushed and overwhelmed. Friends said, "he was utterly broken." He moped, took no interest in life, was out of gear, and then, to the surprise of no one, married again. His son made no protest, knowing that his father was "weak," as it is called, and scarcely responsible, as another would be. He saw, too, that his father "wanted some one to take care of him." But this new wife proved to be a lady of almost frantic extravagance. The castle was refitted and refurnished. She was lavish in balls and entertainments, jewels and dresses; and the Formanton estate, already heavily encumbered, soon began to creak and groan, as it were, like the great dinner-table at one of their banquets, under mortgages and even bills of sale. According to the vulgar phrase, the Formantons were " going it," almost galloping it indeed.

To complete the odd permutations through which Mr. Conway had passed, he had been married. This was known to very few, the truth being that he had lived in that state of life but a few months. He had been married when very young, being not more than one-and-twenty at the time. About this there was a certain romance. His father at the time was only a cousin to the reigning house of Formanton, and had no reasonable chance of succession —such a one, at least, as neither dowager nor money lender of position would for an instant consent to discount. The son of this gentleman, and with but slight chance of advancement in the world, Mr. George Conway would have to fight his way through the world. This he was quite prepared to do, and had the abilities certainly to ensure success. An early romantic attachment to a beautiful young creature might lighten the wearisomeness of the road; but it did not make it smoother when, after many alienations and difficulties, it was known that the handsome, penniless young fellow had married.

However, as we have said, the material consequences of the step were of little moment, for the pretty young creature, frail and delicate, did not linger very long in this world. A few years, the direct line of Formanton became extinct, as the two sons died within a few months of each other, and Mr. George Conway's father became heir to the titles and estates.

One of Mr. Benbow's reasons for desiring to see much of this young man, was the hope of stimulating his son by his example. He cordially admired his easy *degagé* manners and indifference, which he held were of more force as an invitation, and as a lever in securing what you wanted, than any laboured exertion to the same end. But, alas! as he reflected, "this sort of thing" comes by instinct and nature; when assumed, though precisely the same to all appearance, it somehow fails. The casual spectator sees it is counterfeit. If a naturally weak man assumes commanding tones, and requires place to be given to him, the spell will not work in his hands.

Another reason for Mr. Benbow's asking the Formantons, father and son, was, that they were neighbours of his "grand Duke," or "*tres liès*," as some of the fashionable ladies declared it, Formanton and Banff Castle lying close together, the Duke and his Lordship holding the same faith in politics. Both places were at "St. Arthur's-on-Sea," a rising watering-place, created and developed by his Grace, and which, one day or other, would repay the pains and expense bestowed on rearing. Mr. Conway had thus opportunity for indulging in the luxurious taste of yachting and yacht-racing, his boat being

familiar at the various regattas ; while the Duke
and his daughters moved about with a stately
swanlike dignity in their four hundred ton steam
vessel, ' The Lurline.'

This arrival was an additional *agrement* for
his Grace. He had often thought, how suitable
would have been an alliance between his Lady
Rosa and the young heir of Formanton, their
places and estates lying so conveniently together.
And he had done all compatible with dignity
and propriety to " bring it about," as it is called.
The cold Lady Rosa, in her heart of hearts, was
more than kindled by the attractions of Mr.
Conway. Not one of her proposed suitors had
seemed to her so acceptable, and to have so
many gifts that she admired. His many-sided
and uncertain character attracted her and piqued
her. There was nothing of the platitude that
she found in the other young men proposed to
her. Unfortunately she had long seen that Mr.
Conway was wholly indifferent to her. Perhaps
he found in her that very platitude which she
objected to, and that she was but another casting

from the invariable young lady mould. It must not be thought that there was anything of match-making, or the trying to secure a *parti* in these wishes, or the steps taken for their fulfilment. The noble father simply desired to see his daughter established in life, in a suitable station, where she would be happy. Failing Mr. Conway, the Duke's eyes had rested on young Mr. Benbow, a worthy prosaic young fellow, who would make his daughter happy, and would find her a home when he had gone to repose in the vault with preceding dukes. With a sigh, Lady Rosa felt that this must be the course taken, though secretly she hoped that some strange turn might bring about what she wished.

The procession to the state dinner filed down in this order: Mr. Benbow and Lady Rosa; Lord Formanton and the wife of a local baronet; Mr. Conway and the local baronet's daughter; young Mr. Benbow with the clergyman's; the rest, Adelphi guests, according to their degree; and the Duke and a Dowager Peeress. It was all very grand. The state liveries, state

plate, and state lights and flowers. They swept
down. The menials stood to arms as the procession entered those soft realms of delight—all
gleaming with gold and silver, and light, and
flowers. A handsome dinner thus laid out under
the best conditions in a noble mansion; the
table lined with beauty, rank, and wit; the table
itself supporting all that is choice in precious
metals, food and drink; even in its wines stretching far back to some remote " laying down," and
thus keeping up the associations of ancestry: all
this combines to make an *ensemble* that, like the
opera, becomes one of the genuine *shows* of this
earth. The Duke of Banffshire was indeed a
haughty noble. He was a stately man—sur-
prisingly young, and who, by extravagant pains
and diligence, kept himself young, where another
would have looked aged and dilapidated. His
hair was full, brown and curly, his cheeks covered
with a delicate bloom, and he had a haughty and
kingly walk.

Young Mr. Benbow, though " cast " with
another dame, was still placed beside the person

destined for him. Mr. Conway was opposite. How agreeable he was! How he contrived, without effort, to deliver himself of reflections and remarks which always interested! He told stories of himself and his yacht—and somehow there was no air of selfish personality in these disquisitions. Every one was amused or took interest. Mr. Benbow would glance uneasily at his son as he saw that he was eclipsed, and that the Lady Rosa was neglecting her companion for her *vis-à-vis*. The young fellow was good-humoured; and seeing that he was not "making way," was entertaining, as best he could, the clergyman's daughter—and—quite happy.

"By the way," said Mr. Conway, looking round him, "St. Arthur's regatta is coming on, and will be very gay. We expect all the great yachts. Of course you'll be there, Benbow?"

"I hope so," said he, "though the pretty little place is getting spoiled—invaded by the holiday crowds—betting men and riff-raff."

"Ah! that betting, it taints everything; now

it has come to rowing and yachting. Even the pretty Henley is thus disfigured."

Now they are all at the work before them—Mr. Benbow in the centre of the table, so cleanly cast and impassive as to seem above the necessity of eating, and beyond the infirmity of getting flushed or talkative. There is a clatter of gay tongues, and every one is talking of the pleasant party to the theatre to-morrow night. It was pronounced a delightful opportunity, as it was seldom now that one could see a play murdered in the right raw, old-fashioned way. Acting was now levelled up into a sort of stupid, unentertaining mediocrity. The worst actor could contrive, by imitation, a tame, insipid performance, which would neither shock nor please. There was an honest energy in the old, ill-regulated efforts. Claude Melnotte, however, it was agreed, " promised sport," he being played by Mr. Hulkes—the name being " a guarantee."

" Yes," said Mr. Conway, " Hulkes will mouth it and rave it terribly. I shall certainly wait to see Hulkes in 'the immortal Bulwer Lytton's ' play. The manager was very droll; I think he fancied there was a row of footlights between him and us."

"You won't laugh at the Lady of Lyons," said Colonel Hanly, "if she can act as well as she looks."

"Oh, you saw her, then. For shame, Hanly! how sly too!"

"I'll tell you how it was. I was buying a pair of gloves in a shop when she came in with her maid. I know the theatrical seal and hall-mark, stamped on them, or as sheep are stamped. '*You* are the Prima Donna,' I said."

"Come, I say, that was free and easy!"

"Not to her, of course. Charming as an off-the-stage face—a calm, innocent, round face, with an extraordinary fascination. I should have no objection to play Claude, instead of the ranting, roaring Hulkes."

Young Charley Benbow, heir and hope of the house, had been placed close to the Lady Rosa Fulke. It was as though his father had marked out the path to the possession of that lady by stages—so many to be cleared each day. That very dinner was an opportunity, and so much amount of work was to be covered. To say the truth, the lady herself seemed conscious of these elaborate opportunities, and welcomed them with a calm tolerance—a *che farà sarà* air—as though submitting to the decrees of fate and of her noble father.

Her admirer, however, caught this description of the charming Lady of Lyons from afar, and he looked over to hear more. His curiosity was stimulated.

"I heard her speak, too," went on the Colonel—"a beautiful clear voice—and she had all the shopmen at her feet. I saw her name—'Miss Lydia Effingham'—of course a sham one."

"Very likely a runaway clergyman's daughter," said Mr. Conway. "They make up a sort of peculiar class. Whenever you hear anything adventurous, a clergyman's daughter is there. Novelists, actresses, governesses, superior young ladies in Jay's, or Swan and Edgar's, all are generally clergymen's daughters."

In short, this subject was pleasantly debated and speculated over during that night. Anything to look forward to in a country house is always welcome, and this going in state to the little theatre was already counted on as something very piquant.

The young man, who had not as yet gone to the university, and might, as one of his friends said, have passed for a fair girl if dressed up in woman's clothes, was still eager and interested in this theatrical programme. Through his father's desire that he should learn the world rather than books, he had been brought up chiefly at home, with governesses first, then tutors, and finishing with the discipline of a public school. From his infancy almost he had been perpetually brought down when the great magnates were in the house, so that he should grow familiar with them. In this schooling he had seen little of the world after all; for his father considered that theatres and shows of that sort were so many hindrances to getting on. But still the youth, Charles Pelham Benbow, was unsophisticated, rather shy,

and timid, and had not even learned the A B C
of the world's scholar—namely, not to blush.

Nay, his father, who considered that effects
in his diplomacy followed causes with accuracy
and certainty, gave him his lesson in portions,
as it were, guaranteeing the result—taking care
also to examine him closely afterwards. The
youth was astonished himself at the wonderful
fashion in which his father penetrated things.

The cold lady he was destined for was quite
indifferent as to his partiality or attentions. Her
noble father, who had so often dealt with his
tenants as chattels about election time, was now
about to follow the same course with her. That
was all. She had gone through her *curriculum*,
which had been a failure. Her glass told her
she could not afford to waste time in beginning
again, and she wisely preferred to retire with
dignity.

After dinner came one of the state evenings at
Benbow House. Spacious rooms, opening into
each other; abundant, profuse wax lights; company sitting, standing, scattered; loud and

boisterous talk from a group on the rug; his Grace sitting as on a throne, one leg out, the other under his chair, his Thistle ribbon across his chest, while two ladies sat one on each side. He was the wonder of every one: his florid Rubens-like face and beard, his "young man's" head of hair, divided in the middle, his good eyes, erect carriage. Yet he had grown-up sons and daughters, and was a grandfather many times over.

Presently he rose and went over to join his starched and bleached host, who still looked, and always would look, as if cast in snowy *papier mâché*, so clean and sharp were his lines; and far off, in the small card-room, there was presently seen a trio—the Duke, the father, and the son, talking; the latter modestly looking down, while the two parents spoke as if to encourage him.

"Charles has promised to come back with us," said the Duke, "and must stay six weeks or two months. I mean you must first fix your head-quarters with us, and come and go as you like. I shall come and go myself *sans cérémonie;* but her Grace and Rosa will always be there."

Had Mr. Benbow's soul been cased in any other material but *papier mâché*, a flush of pleasure and delight would have found its way to his face; for this was one of the little explosions for which his elaborate mine was laid.

The invitation was accepted instantly and joyfully.

"We shall make a political man of him," went on the Duke; "I shall do a little of his training myself. The Duchess and Rosa are both politicians *enragées*. Nothing like being a thorough 'party-man,' even when you are *not* a man."

"Lady Rosa is looking for her fan, Charles," said his father. "See there! go and help her."

When the young man had flown—"I like your son," said the Duke, "and shall like him much more. I don't ask you myself to Banff Castle this time; you will come later, of course —at your own convenience. As I told you, I shall not be there; but young men do not care if there is only a lady to do the honours. Rosa and he get on very well."

" No one admires Lady Rosa Fulke and her accomplishments more," said Mr. Benbow, as if he were making a legal statement.

" Yes, I hope they will get on well together."

Precious words these for Mr. Benbow—to be eaten, drunk of, dreamed of—words long looked for, thirsted for, and, to him, more than equivalent to—" I have thought it well over, and have decided to accept Charles as my son-in-law."

That night there was the usual ballad song—the pianoforte piece from the clergyman's daughter. The Lady Rosa went to " the instrument " also—(" Why is that called 'the instrument,'" said Mr. Conway, " any more than the poker or tongs, or the pier-table ?")—and literally ambled, in a very humble way over the keys, some little thing which she had been taught by Pesca, the nobility's own pianist, but who was instructing the royal children. Then Mr. Charles, the candidate, stood by her side as an escort. It was a very indifferent performance, but redeemed by the calm, aristocratic repose of the player, who made even her wrong notes with an air of self-possession.

Mr. Conway appeared to appreciate and like Lady Rosa, and praised her singing with cordiality. Had he *really* liked her, she thought, one of his character would have been more restrained and chary of his praise.

"I am glad it pleases you," she said. "I know you are *difficile*."

"That was the thought that was in my mind about you, Lady Rosa," he said, laughing, "about another matter. That poor young Benbow. He really means his praises, and speaks out of the fulness of his heart. I do not—often, that is—though I do wish it."

"These refinements of yours are hard to follow," she said.

"All my fault," he answered.

"You *are* a puzzling character, it must be confessed."

"Yes, yes; indeed I am. I often wonder how I shall end."

"Oh, I suppose prosperously," said she, lightly. "Everything is sure to turn out well with you. If things are not inclined of themselves to do, people will make them."

He drew his chair close to hers and sat down. They often had these friendly confidential "talks" at Banff.

"No, no," he said seriously; "I have no such idea. People talk of fate, which is of course absurd, meaning by fate a power compelling you to take a course. But I believe there is a fate in ourselves—in our own capricious moods and tenses—which entangle us in strange ways and places. I have always an idea that I may bring distress and suffering to others if not to myself; how or wherefore I know not."

Lady Rosa answered him gravely:

"I should think that is not at all unlikely. Indeed it has often occurred to me."

"If it has," he said, now interested, "there must be a reason. Tell me, and you will oblige me. Tell me frankly what you think of my character."

"I!" said she, haughtily. "What! flatter

you in that way. No, no. Excuse me. Go to the phrenologists for that."

Here arrives Mr. Benbow, with his son. He had been watching uneasily from afar.

" Charles is dying for another song," he said.

" Yes, indeed," said the latter, " if Lady Rosa would be so kind."

And she was ; for she went over to " the instrument," and performed again.

But now it was growing late. The party began to break up, as did also, strangely, the young-looking Duke, as the late hours drew on. Then trays and glasses were brought in ; powdered menials flitting about, and a general uprising and flutter as the personage left the room, attended devoutly by the master of the house.

In the august chamber they had some talk about " the party," and on wishing good-night his Grace said :

" We must make a good party man of your son Charles. We'll try and do that when we have him at Banff. I assure you we all like him very much."

CHAPTER III.

AT Dipchester the Theatre Royal was a very modest house of entertainment, and perhaps deserved the term of contempt which some of the profession were fond of applying to it—viz. its being " a wretched band-box of a thing." It had a pleasant, old-fashioned air. The boxes or galleries had fallen rather out of shape; the pit was little bigger than a goodly-sized cockpit; and there was a genuine old green curtain, of the true coarse tone, which has so long ago gone out. But in full force there was the true bouquet or flavour of rank gas, or sawdust, drifting down little tunnels of passages, all ablaze with flaring lights — a bouquet which is enjoyed most in purely country theatres; which, could their old walls speak, whether now turned into Dissenters' chapels or corn stores, could tell of more real enjoyment and heartier laughter than ever rose through the stately "auditorium" of a London house.

A little crowd was round the doors. A meagre awning sloped down over the little cabin-stairs of the chief entrance, and some tar was blazing in bowls at each side. There was a glimpse through the narrow door of some striped red calico, and at times a glimpse of the interior of the house itself; for one all but passed from the street into the boxes.

Here at last was the sound of wheels, and here were three carriages of company from Benbow dashing up—their lamps like dragons' eyes, their footmen in long cloaks, and panels gleaming like armour. Out came Mr. Haggerston, bursting from behind the pink and white calico—as he had burst often before, on false alarms—and received the august party at the foot of the little cabin-stairs. Down they were set—the stately Duke and his host, both—ribbons across, clouds of tulle and flowers on ducal daughter; while the cheerful young men of the party bounded out of the small brougham that brought up the tail of the procession, not caring about being squeezed. The little steps—much decayed—creaked under the ducal feet, while Mr. Haggerston, in full dress, led the way round the squeezed little passage to the extemporised private box next the stage—striped calico attending them all the way; and there a gaunt servant in a faded stage livery, who had brought in more " dummy " letters than he had ever done real ones, crouched against the wall. The little interior was crowded. Every eye in that first curve—which held about six boxes — was turned to the distinguished party, and the five musicians in the little pen called the orchestra struck up a complimentary tune. It was really " a grand night " for the theatre, such as it had never known before, and was fondly looked back to by the manager and his company; for what with extra lighting, and cleaning, and calico, the little house had never looked so festive.

The august—almost royal—party were late, and had kept the audience waiting. So bills were at once placed before them, when the party, with many smiles, saw that their own names had been made "to draw" as well as the players'. It was all "under the distinguished patronage of his Grace the Duke of Banffshire; Spencer Pelham Benbow, Esq., of Benbow Castle; Charles Benbow, Esq.; and the Right Hon. J. Hoxter." They also read that Pauline, in the cast of the "immortal Bulwer Lytton," was to be played by Miss Lydia Effingham, and Claude by Mr. Hulkes, of the Theatres Royal, Plymouth and Dorking. But where was the agreeable Conway? Alas! "Loaves and Fishes" had a headache, and could not go. Mr. Conway, indifferent to the play and to Lady Rosa, declared he would stay. But the ladies were so disappointed that he agreed to go.

The august visitors found great entertainment in looking round the house, and in identifying the curious figures that were clustered there. Stalls had been laid out in even the pit, which only left three or four rows of seats for the regular clients; but the people to whom they were sacrificed had their punishment in strained necks, twisted round all the night long to the left, to observe the movements of the august party. There was no tendency to laugh at any rusticity in these honest folk of the district, as vulgar in great people as the vulgarity they are amused at; but young Charles Benbow, seated by the Lady Rosa—carrying out his special duty —gave the names of the figures seated round, and little sketches. That night might have been a favourable opportunity for completing his father's darling scheme; but that cautious diplomatist thought the aristocratic pear not yet ripe, and had carefully warned his son not to precipitate matters. It had been better had he let events take their own course: all then had been well for him, and this little narrative not been written.

The youth, in truth, flattered by a consideration which was new to him, was eager; and in that light, and the excitement of the evening, invested

her with charms which were not her own. She,
too, was pleased with his natural and boyish
homage, and smiled a natural smile as he gave
the names and recounted little histories of the
neighbours about them. Thus, in the private
box opposite, that florid-faced, coarse-looking
young man, with diamond studs, was young
Hunter, who had not long come in for the great
cotton mills—a vulgar-minded upstart—who was
sitting there with two " flappers," run in the
same mould, beside him. His creed in life was
to get everything by *paying*, and by paying the
largest price. That large party in the centre
was the Muggeridge family, leading people of the
town : he, the rich local solicitor ; she, a great,
oval-shaped, crimson egg—flaming in face, and
flowers, and opera-cloak — surrounded with a
family of coloured Easter eggs. Then there was
the doctor's family ; the clergyman's daughters
—who, on this occasion, waived the severe
principles of their profession, and came to see
the rare spectacle of a duke in the theatre. But
hush ! now the curtain had gone up, and " the

immortal Bulwer Lytton" and his play set in.

The young and too presumptuous Claude—the " Gee-ardener's son," as he was called through the piece, and he could not fairly complain, as he so spake of himself—was discovered to be rather elderly, his bare throat displayed in a boyish fashion, which only exhibited a disagreeable, crude redness, and the cordage of muscles. This gentleman's rapturous juvenility and amorousness were diverting enough, and a smile came on the ducal features as he bade his mother " embrace her boy."

But all was expectation as the scene opened where the new Pauline was expected to come on. Faces were turned eagerly to the stage ; and a charming, distinguished-looking girl, with bright eyes, and dressed with as much taste and propriety as if she were going to a ball, came on modestly and slowly. A torrent of applause welcomed her. It was renewed as she made a curtsey — half indifferent, half gracious, and wholly unstagy. Her face beamed with a bright intelligence; and the contrast of her own pure self with the tawdry dresses, the smirched faces of those about, and even the dirty and rickety background, made her look like a princess visiting a hovel.

The Duke said to his neighbour, "Quite a lady!—you can know one when we see her."

The Lady Rosa's pale face bore a smile of disdain and hostility, while Mr. Hoxter and the gentlemen applauded boisterously. But the young Benbow kept his eyes fixed on her, as on some vision — his cheeks glowing, his pulses fluttering. He had never seen or even dreamed of anything so lovely or entrancing as she appeared to him.

The play went on; the Gee-ardener's son, now all velvet and spangles, striding about and mouthing round the beautiful heroine, seeming like her groom—and a dirty one too—dressed up in finery; and General (Haggerston) Damas delivered his military jokes with a strange in-attention to his companions, always keeping his face twisted round to the right, and addressing his speeches entirely to the Duke—the Duke of the audience. When the attractive Pauline spoke, what a tingling music rang through the house! how ears were drooped to catch every sound! In the scene where our groom "Gee-ardener" had brought her to a home, which corresponded to the one Mr. Hulkes personally was more familiar with, what passionate upbraidings, what charming gestures, as she covered her face with her veil and sank down and wept! Then her cry of anguish, as Mr. Hulkes rushed away to the wars, made Mr. Hoxter turn round to the Duke, and say, seriously, "This is very fine, really very fine"—much as he would turn round in another House and praise a new speaker. Young Benbow, as the act finished, put his hands forward over the box and applauded noisily; while even the Lady Rosa had a faint flush on her cheeks, and said, "She reminded her a little of Madalene Droze." One only of the party was uninterested—Mr. Benbow —whose quick, bright eye roved from face to face of his party, and, noticing his son's enthusiasm, he moved quietly down into the seat behind him.

"Nothing so wonderful, Lady Rosa," he said; "and Charles has seen little or no acting"—and at the same moment gave him a firm and quiet pressure with his finger.

Now there is a roar of applause, demanding the favourite; while Mr. Hulkes, scowling and in ill-humour, comes out by himself; and, when he has disappeared, Mr. Haggerston, in person, and in the full uniform of General Damas (which suggests the idea that British officers were serving with the French armies), leads in the charming actress. She is now very different— sweeps across with a chilling *hauteur*—a kind of unresponsive indifference—as if she cared nothing for them or their tributes.

A hurried dialogue passed in the " royal " box.

" We should throw her a bouquet," said Mr. Hoxter.

The General Officer on the stage—who had never taken his eyes off the distinguished party, in a fixed and stony gaze—guessed what was passing, and lingered; while the eager Charles, standing up, frantically applauded.

She gave a gracious curtsey in acknowledgment, and disappeared; whilst the youth remained standing—his hands on the front of the box, he himself in a sort of enraptured abstraction.

"How splendid! How magnificent!" he said at last. "Wasn't it? I never saw anything to approach it."

He then got up suddenly and left the box. His father looked round hastily as the door closed; but he was too late. There was a general chorus of approbation in that circle, and Mr. Hoxter declared loudly she ought to be "in town."

CHAPTER IV.

THE young man, once out in the corridor, fanned his excited face with his handkerchief; then, with hesitation, tapped at a side-door which led on to the stage. He asked for Mr. Haggerston, and found that gentleman still in the full regimentals of a General of Division—which seemed all tri-colour sash, boots, and breeches—and giving impetuous orders to his dependants, as if he were indeed upon the field of battle.

"There's a triumph! There's genius! Mr. Benbow. That went home to my lord Duke's soul. I saw it. I know it did."

"They were all delighted, Haggerston. By the way, I was going to ask you, would you mind—" and he dropped his voice and whispered.

"To be sure. Perfect lady, you know. Rather touchy, in fact, about these sort of things though But I'll speak to her."

Mr. Haggerston presently returned, and led the way to a little crib known as the dressing-room.

Pauline rose up to receive them; while a grave lady, older by ten years than she was, looked on with suspicion. Mr. Haggerston then performed an introduction after the manner he knew best.

"Here you are, Miss Effingham, young Mr. Benbow is dying to know you. Regular swell," he half-whispered.

The lady started at the name.

The youth, now that he was close beside her, saw that she had a natural, everyday loveliness, far beyond what he had seen in her on the stage. He felt the very blood rushing to his heart and cheeks.

"I was so enchanted," he faltered, "so interested, that I could not take my eyes away a moment."

"I remarked you," she said, smiling at this natural confusion. "You were in that box to the right. Your steady interested look made me play better."

"Oh, it makes me so *proud* to hear that, Miss Effingham. I forgot the theatre, and where I was, and who I was with."

"Who was that lady next you—so cold and indifferent to my poor exertions? Only for you I should have been quite paralyzed by her."

"The Duke's daughter, Lady Rosa Fulke. She has seen so many plays, you will understand, Miss Effingham—"

"Yes. They all know the 'Lady of Lyons' by heart. You have seen it a thousand times."

"No, indeed; never before. But if you, Miss Effingham, act it a thousand times here, I shall go every night. How long will you stay?"

"A fortnight. Of course, contingent—" and she smiled. "The doors of these country theatres sometimes shut so very abruptly. But you are really pleased with me? What can I do here? I might as well act in a drawing-room. I want room, space, air—the vast stage, like a great field; and, far away, the dim, lofty —not *sea*, but *cloud*, of faces rising up. Oh, if I had that chance, Mr. Benbow, you would see something very different from what you see to-night."

"Oh, I have seen acting," the young man said, eagerly; "but could not see anything finer than yours!"

"There was one face besides yours that I noted," she said. "It was the only one of the rest that seemed to follow and sympathize."

"Oh, I know," said the young man, eagerly. "It's just what I would expect. That was Conway."

"I shall remember his name," she said, reflectively, "with yours. He is your friend too, I am certain."

"He is; he is," said Charles, enthusiastically; "and you will like him when you know him."

Mr. Haggerston struck in—"Miss Effingham

literally brought the house down. I kept my eye on his Grace when I was joking you in the garden scene, and every point seemed to go home to him, you know. I assure you, you were tip-top; and — do me justice, Miss Effingham —I led well up to you."

She seemed to shrink away from these compliments.

" I was not thinking of any person—of dukes or any one else ; and, to tell you the truth, I am more pleased with the simple praise this gentleman has bestowed on me, than with any of the compliments which I suppose will be sent to me after this is over."

A tap at the door.

This conversation might, under other conditions, have seemed a very strange and odd one—Mr. Haggerston—wearing his false moustache and beard—so palpably stuck on—his coarse stage uniform, sash, &c. But Charles was in a sort of dream, and even delirium— his eyes fixed on the features of the beautiful actress.

The knock at the door was repeated impatiently.

General Damas leisurely went and " threw it open," as he would call it.

The coarse young manufacturer stood there, in the glory of his chains, rings, &c., and bowing and smirking.

" Beg pardon, Haggerston," he said ; " just want you to do a bit of the polite. Introduce me to the charming and fascinating young lady who has been obliging us all to-night."

Mr. Haggerston did what was desired, with intense enthusiasm.

" Delighted, my dear sir. Mr. Hunter, Miss— a true patron of the drama, and of everything that belongs to it."

" Oh come, I say, Hag—put in discriminating. You never get a five shillings out of me when you have any of your common lot of people coming round. But I declare, when you secure such an attraction—such as Miss Heffingam—"

The haughty look, mingled with contempt,

which he received, checked this flow of compliment. She then turned to Charles.

"There, you hear the invariable sort of praise I always receive. You would be surprised at the number of times I have heard it."

"I say, Hag," went on the other, not in the least abashed, "you'll have to raise the pay and allowances; and don't you spare him, Miss Effingham—he's rolling in money."

"Mr. Haggerston's arrangements and mine have been already settled," she said, quite gravely. "I have no wish to change them."

"Oh, that was only my fun, you know," said the objectionable young manufacturer, "and only what I would do if I were Haggerston. I wish I was. I think a cool hundred a week would be the least *I'd* offer you."

The young man had been listening impatiently. He had the slight acquaintance with the manufacturer which every one in or about a country town has to form and keep up. He could not restrain himself any longer; but said, with flushing cheeks:

"No one is thinking of these commercial views. Miss Effingham does not care about them."

"It is rather hard," she added, "considering all that is before me in the next acts. This gentleman takes away all the poetry of my art from me."

"Oh, well," said Mr. Hunter, much put out, "that is what you all look to, you know, in the profession."

"Yes," said Charles, "by one sort—the people who make it a trade."

"Oh, I 'ate those chaffering, peddling fellows that come to me sometimes," said Mr. Haggerston, heartily endorsing this sentiment. "No one has an idea the way we managers are victimised; we are literally poorer than the fellow there that I employ to sweep my stage. We never get a real good bargain; for, if they make ever so little of a success, then they turn greedy—greedy; want two pounds a week more —may be, this very night before the drop is down, on just some twopenny-halfpenny calls which I here vow to you I get up myself. I assure you, the meanness, the dirt—the absolute dirt, sir—that's in the profession, you wouldn't believe! Bless my soul, but you can't stay talking here, and keep his Grace waiting. Now then, Miss Effingham, when you're ready I am."

"Let me offer you my arm, Miss Effingham," said young Mr. Benbow, "and bring you to the wing."

Mr. Hunter was abashed and angry. He could buy and sell young Benbow, and, for that matter—as he said to his friend later in the boxes—any strolling actress like that. He was dreadfully put out.

"I'll give her a lesson yet, and that cock-sparrow too. But she *is* infernal handsome!" And under his elaborately-worked shirt-front, his swinging gold chains, and glossy suit, he was mortified. Deeply touched with her charms, he told his admiring friend and flapper—quite after the nature of his kind—that "she was a tip-top splendid girl."

"And you made the running," said a flapper. "Don't tell me—she was making eyes at you all the time of the play!"

Clumsy as this sort of compliment is, most men can understand it; and, though his rebuff was rankling in his mind, he gave way to the pleasant delusion that some such gratifying success as had been described had actually taken place.

CHAPTER V.

As young Mr. Benbow led the actress through the dark places by the edge of the scenes, peopled with what seemed unclean spectres, the pride and fluttering of his heart was indescribable. He felt that he was, as it were, leading some rich and rare Queen, far greater than any of the Deschappelles family ; and he found himself standing with her, a sudden and dazzling glare pouring in upon him. Then some one came and whispered her ; and in a moment he found himself alone — heard the sudden burst of applause, as it were, at a distance—and knew that the enchanting Pauline was again entangled in that passionate love adventure, of which, alas !—and a thousand times alas !—he was not the hero. That dreadful, dirty, scrubby, degraded Hulkes, to dare, even by the necessities of stage action, to assume the character of even a sham lover!

In the glare of this coarse stage light he was standing, his eyes fixed on her who now absorbed his whole soul; but he never thought that he was in full view of the box where the august party were sitting. When, for a moment or two, he had withdrawn his gaze from the divine creature who was so gallantly cleaving to the absent "Gee-ardener's son"—then winning his grade under the French flag—he became conscious that he had been in full view of the distinguished persons in the box; and thought, with some confusion, of his father, who might have seen him leading the charming actress to the wing.

He hurried round at once to take his place in the box, and stole as softly as he could into his own place.

"We saw you," said the Duke's daughter frigidly; "you seem to have acquaintances behind the scenes."

"Not at all," he said, hurriedly. "It was only that Haggerston, who would introduce me."

"Introduce you!" she repeated, scornfully; "and is *that* done behind the scenes?"

Without looking back, he felt—and felt most uncomfortably—that his father's eyes were on him, piercing into his very skull. He made a feint at exaggerated devotion and eager attention; but all the time the entrancing Pauline's history was going on; and here was that odious Hulkes, returned from the wars, hiding his ill-rasped cheeks—as every Claude invariably does or tries to do—behind that enormous Colonel's plume of white feathers. There had been a sweet constancy about her, a gentle womanly tenderness indescribable; filial to her parents—Mr J. S. Webb and Mrs. Charles Walterby—and enduring the hearty jesting of that old officer, General Haggerston Damas; and now she was flying into the arms of Hulkes with a woman's passionate enthusiasm.

Charles could not think of any Duke's daughter

then. As the applause broke out, he forgot all his father's splendid plans, and, turning eagerly to his companions, said :

"And look, look, she only *appears* to embrace him. How cleverly done ! She is a true lady, and does not allow that fellow's dirty fingers to touch her dress even. Haggerston assures me that a real nice actress will not allow such a thing. There is 'lady' stamped upon her in everything she does."

The Lady Rosa turned in her seat to look at him, with a stare of astonishment.

"How can I know anything of these people and their ways ! You talk of ladies—I believe no lady could bring herself to go on a stage like that !"

There, it was over—the curtain down, and the audience calling for that divine creature. Mr. Hunter was "roaring for her," and clapping, standing up in his box, young Mr. Benbow noticed, as she was coming out, led by Mr. Haggerston.

Again an uprising—a cheering.

Mr. Hoxter said again, "I declare we ought to throw her a bouquet. If Covent-garden were near, she would deserve a guinea one."

Charles again forgot all that was about him, and the duty before him. He heard these words. "Oh, yes," he said, eagerly, "we must throw her one. It will be too late, if we are not quick." He stooped down, scarcely knowing what he was doing. "Would you eternally oblige me — let me take yours now, and to-morrow the finest that Covent-garden—"

"By all means; it was you who gave it to me, so you have the right—"

Only a second more, and the divine apparition would have disappeared. Some one was holding aside the old green baize "rag." He could not have checked himself if it was to save himself from death.

"Oh, thank you, thank you," he said; and, seizing the bouquet, threw it.

It landed at her feet. Mr. Haggerston bounded at it, and took it up in the laboriously gallant way which is *de rigueur* on these occasions. It was presented to her, and she curtseyed, as Mr. Hoxter owned, "like a lady. Certainly a clergyman's daughter—commonest thing in the world."

The Duke laughed — he was mentally short-sighted—and said, "See, Rosa has made him throw her bouquet."

It was over. The august party were not going to wait for the afterpiece, even though the funny man — the leading *comique* of the theatre—was going to give his Jeremy Diddler— his great part. August parties never wait for afterpieces — as, indeed, Mr. Haggerston good-naturedly prophesied to his *comique*. As they all rose—every eye in the theatre on them— some of the local fashionables felt it would be provincial and unbecoming to remain, and so they began to rise also; and the unhappy *comique* had to play his great part to a very thin audience indeed, chiefly aloft.

Mr. Haggerston was in attendance, having made a frantic toilet to be in time; the stage servant was in waiting, and unrolling an old bit of stage-carpeting; there was the plunging of horses and drawing-up of carriages. Then they drove away; and the great bespeak performance, long talked of in the theatre, was over.

CHAPTER VI.

IN MR. BENBOW'S STUDY.

AFTER the distinguished party had reached home, and retired for the night, Mr. Benbow said quietly to his son, "Come to my study, Charles, before you go to bed;" and then went himself to hold communion with his papers, as was his wont.

Those were strange, troubled vigils of his: like some necromancer, he called up spirits, and peopled the air about him with spectres bearing coronets, and heard mysterious cries of "Lord!" and "Viscount!" "Premier!" "M.P.!" and "Minister!" It was like the dark cellars below the great electric telegraph stations, where are the great troughs and batteries, and from whence the fluid leaps away to all the ends of the earth.

The young man, a little uneasy at this appointment, kept his young men friends up as long as he could—where he received that most unwelcome "chaffing" on his visit behind the scenes—then went and knocked at his father's door.

That worn, restless face looked up from a vast embankment of papers, and from overflowing drawers.

"Come in, Charles," he said; "take a chair. Have you shut the outside door?"

The son, much confused, did so. He knew that this was a fatal symptom of something serious. When he had returned to his place, the father sat back in his chair, and, putting his fingers together so as to make his arms and hands seem like a pair of compasses, began quietly:

"You are a fool, I fear!"

The son hung down his head.

"Do you hear me? Are you a fool, or are you sensible? Or are you resolved to take a course of your own?"

He paused.

"See, I must have an answer to these two questions, and a plain one. If you feel that you are so imbecile as to be unequal to taking your part in a scheme which I am arranging for your good, say so distinctly, and save me much weary trouble. I ask you again, do you feel yourself a fool?"

"No, no, father; I hope not."

"Then give some sensible explanation of your behaviour to-night. Take your time."

"I assure you, my dear father—"

His father's eyes were fixed on him, with a patient and hard air. He was really waiting an explanation.

"It was only—that is—I just went behind the scenes—as any young man would do."

"You *are* a fool," said his father, with strong emphasis. "I see it—a great one."

"Oh, I hope not."

"Then you must not attempt to do anything for yourself. You have nearly destroyed my whole plan. Do you not know the cost, the labour, the anxiety of years—yes, sir, of years—that I have been at, to bring matters to this stage? and you go on like a child with a drum and a cart. Now, I have sent for you to give you a plain warning. These are *my* plans, not yours. If you oppose them in any way, I shall do with you as I have done with every one —in or outside of my family—who has dared not to co-operate with me. I have turned them out, cast them aside, and got others. And I'll do it to you. I can get a substitute for you any day. You know that I do what I say, and have done what I said. Look at this bundle of letters I came on to-night—wife begging mercy, daughter begging—he himself: all of no use. Go, now; that's all. Do your best to-morrow to repair your bungling of to-night, or else—— Good night. Go!"

The youth withdrew, much relieved. But when he got to his room, the walls seemed to open and float away to each side, disclosing the scene of Paradise—the soft clouds which encompassed that one divine figure—the sweet smile—the bright and glorious face, whose glance lit up his very soul. Her enchanting tones still rang in his ears like music. Her passionate gestures, her loving manner, her devotion—when she rushed to the arms of the gardener's son. But that he could not bear to think of. To be profaned by the touch of a Hulkes! Oh, that *he* could have been the Claude—what fire, what passion he would throw into it! Let his father talk of striving for peerages and political position for which he was struggling—those miserable dry husks—what were they to *that* prize? As he pursued this dream, watching that vision, listening to that divine music, his father's stiff figure and cold face passed away; and he gave himself up to a delicious rapture, and feasted again and again on those Paradisaical visions.

His father, after some measured walking round the room, came back to his interrupted work. "How dare he?" he said to himself, as he sat down. "The idiot, the booby—with his low music-hall fancies. Why, I don't know

that he has not ruined everything as it is. No;
but I cannot have mistaken him. His tutors,
all—I see it myself—they agreed that he was
a steady, plodding lad. He *must* be," added the
father, aloud, with a sort of agony; "it wants
little more to the end. Another day only. I
paved the whole road for him: he has but to
walk straight forward, and lean on me. Oh, he
must!"

He turned to his papers again.

"How curious my coming on these to-night."
And he struck the small bundle with the open
palm of his hand.

"Ah, you, sir, tried the same game with me
years ago; and I crushed you, just as I might
stand with my whole weight on some beetle.
Yes," he added, turning over one letter, "this
was his wife's appeal—a despairing one, I
recollect."

He then read it half aloud:

"'For God's sake, Mr. Benbow, have pity on
us, and let not his ruin be on your soul. After
all, it was but a moment's folly or sin; and you

ruined him first. He was weak, guilty, cruel ;
but has he not atoned for it ? Have we not all
suffered terrible privation ? I tell you we are
starving. I conjure you, leave us in peace, and
do not so pitilessly hinder us from living, or
drive us out like pariahs from every place where
we settle down. Surely, sir, you know that
men of the first rank, in all their bitterness of
hate, have never brought this animosity into
their private dealings. Oh, as you will be
judged hereafter, forget—forgive ! Think of
him—think of me—of my poor, beautiful,
tender girl ! Don't hunt me down.' "

He paused, then said scornfully :

" His principles ! Mine are those of justice
and no mercy. Every creature driven to the
wall, as it is called—the wretch who is to be
hanged to-morrow—is penitent enough : ' *They
will never do it again.*' Of course not. But
they would. And here is *your* letter, sir : ' You
are too noble, and too generous, and have been
too successful in your career, to think of reveng-
ing yourself on one so humble as I am. We

have been enemies, and I have done my best—I own it. You will respect me the more for owning it. Further, you will respect me still more when I tell you that I would have died rather than submit to the humiliation of asking you for anything; but I am not stoical enough to see my poor girl suffer. Now you have an opportunity of being victorious over *me*, and of using your victory generously. For the sake of Heaven—in a lower degree, for the sake of pity and humanity—not for me, for I shall not long survive this part of the disgrace—spare us! or you will feel bitter remorse. More—our ruin will rise up one day in another shape against you, mark me! We know it is revenge.'"

He looked at it for a long time, steadily, then laid it down.

"It would not—could not be," he said, slowly. "As well stop the wheels of a Juggernaut. Mine had to go over him; and it was well I did what I did."

He seized the bundle of letters, tied them hastily, and flinging them into a drawer—

heaping others over them—closed it with a crash. Then the sject was gone from his mind; but he remained—his head on his hands, his eyes fixed on a spot of carpet near the door.

"If this boy of mine should fail me in any way! But not one of them can be depended on. No one is like myself. All—all helpless, more or less. The fool."

Then he remembered that there were letters—meshes of various spiders' webs—to be written—half-a-dozen and more—to go by the morning's post. These he wrote. It was three by the Benbow clock when he had done, and walked into a little room off his own, where there was a small brass bedstead, and then tried to sleep.

Such was Mr. Benbow, who, every one said, was a very ambitious man. So he was.

With the morning, the master of the house was up and abroad betimes—indeed, with the gardener, giving him some most minute directions.

Just as the guests were coming in to breakfast, he called his son to him again, and spoke to him calmly

"Recollect I shall see and hear you, everywhere, and at any time," he said, "though you may not think it."

When Lady Rosa came in, the young man walked up to her, and, with the true blush of the *ingenuus puer*, bent before her with a splendid bouquet, and said :

"I hope you will accept this, Lady Rosa, in place of the one I robbed you of last night. It was a sudden impulse, and I was carried away by the play."

His father came up softly. Her father smiled. Mr. Benbow's arm went round the shoulders of his son.

"Charles has been to few theatres. Why, when I was his age I could hardly keep still in my place when I saw the 'Castle Spectre.' What is like Hassan's dream, after all? I could say it now. I recollect I was quite dazzled by a plain Miss Smith."

The daughter laughed.

"I envy you, if you have not seen plays. I confess I am tired of them. When he is with us in town, he shall be taken to a regular course, and disenchanted."

Mr. Benbow, the father, struck in again, adroitly.

"His sympathies were so excited. And it *is* an exciting story. He was talking of it to me for an hour in the study. He felt so for that poor Pauline, separated from her lover."

Then Mr. Benbow turned to the Duke, to talk of the distinguished author.

"What a very remarkable man he is—something of Sheridan about him. Dramatist, poet, novelist, orator, diplomatist, and minister!"

"Sheridan wrote no novels," said the Duke, much pleased at the opportunity for correction, which Mr. Benbow might have left for him purposely.

"No; no more he did," he said, in surprise. "That gives a superiority to Lytton."

"And I am not aware that Sheridan wrote any parliamentary satirical poem—say of the character of ' St. Stephen's.' "

"No; he certainly did not. You are quite

right, Duke.   Oh, the modern writer is certainly the most versatile."

Some such little weapons as these were always ready in the Benbow armoury, much as some careful lady would carry about a " housewife " in her pocket.   These and much more were part of the laborious machinery he was working, to try and repair the damage of last night.   And when, about lunch-time, the Duke, addressing Charles, said good-humouredly, " I suppose the attractions of the stage will not keep you away from us," his father considered that all had been restored.

He called Charles aside, and bade him go out and ride, and never leave the side of Lady Rosa for his life.

" There, you goose !   I have repaired the mischief done by your folly of last night, and forgive you ; but *mind*, take care it never happens again.   I say, attend to me.   Take care that nothing like it happens again."   This with a fierce look.

CHAPTER VII.

A LOVER.

THE young Charles, thoroughly scared, put on a laborious devotion to the lady allotted to him. But he was carrying about a leaden heart. All about him seemed dark, and laid in dull, gloomy colours; but, as he would look out afar—beyond —to where was the soft light, the white clouds, the plaintive music, the bright angelic face, he felt his heart aching and sinking, a sense of despair and blankness coming over him, and he loathed the part he was playing. He longed to fling away all restraint, hurry out of the place, rush to the stable, and ride off headlong to the little town—to the theatre, where the play would soon be beginning, and the divine Pauline having her affections a second time won by the odious Hulkes.

But he must do something to quiet his soul—
the agitating flutter in his breast. Action of
any kind in such cases is an advance forward,
and may bring something to disturb the wearing
monotony of expectancy. He would write something—something complimentary. It would be
next to sight or speech. It seemed like an
inspiration, and he wrote:

"DEAR MISS EFFINGHAM,
　　　　　"That delightful 'last night'
is still before me. Your enchanting tones
are still in my ears. *I never saw or heard
anything to approach what I saw and heard last
night!* I never shall forget it. It seems like a
sweet dream. Here they are still talking of it.
All the judges say there was nothing ever
like it. You seemed the real Pauline; and, oh!
I think that odious Hulkes was very happy in
being allowed to *imitate* even one who was
allowed to adore you. If you would let me call
upon you, and tell you all I think, and how
delighted I was, it will be a great happiness to,
yours always,

"CHARLES PELHAM BENBOW."

He felt much better and more at ease when he sent this off by a secret hand—an uncouth stable-boy, who was his serf. Now he had something to look forward to — her answer. But none was to come as yet.

His father watched him the whole day.

In a sort of fevered flutter—half distressing, half delightful—the young man endured this *espionage*. Once more he thought of rushing to the stable, leaping on his horse, and galloping off furiously into Dipchester. His blood was in a fever; he could not rest calmly in one spot; and his enforced squireship of the aristocratic young lady was hateful to him. There was an over-acting, an over-eagerness in playing his part, which he made almost passionate in his attention and devotion.

His plan at the beginning of the day, and to which he always looked forward with a sort of painful yearning, had been to absent himself for two or three hours, and see his charmer. But, with that ever vigilant police, it became impossible. There was the morning, then lunch, then the ride; and his father, looking warily to the grand object he then had on hand, posted him duly, as a sergeant would sentries. And so that wretched dragging day went by until the dinner came round—the old regular state form—a time of agony for him; for he knew that the curtain was up, and the enchanting Pauline again showing her love for the sham prince, and passing through those cruel trials.

Still, with this weight at his heart, he acquitted himself respectably; and his father gravely commended him, made a sort of formal apology for his words of last night, and now said that he had a great deal of sense.

"My dear boy," he said, with some warmth, "wait—only wait until you see what I shall do for you. We shall be the greatest family in England yet. You don't know—it can't enter into your head to conceive—all that I have planned—all the engines working at this moment. They little dream what schemes are in this head. You shall be a marquis when I am gone. Not that I care for a bare title;

but POWER is the thing.　Power, Charles—power is only got by connection. This Duke is a stupid man, but see what power he has : simply by the force of accumulated connection. Once let us weld on our family to his,. and his connections are mine ! It wants a clever man to put it all to use. I am that man. And now, my dear boy, as you have shown sense, I shall speak plainly to you. The sole and only difficulty in the way is the girl herself. She requires delicate management. Her father even can scarcely control her. She is cold and obstructive, and should she see the least backwardness or indifference in you, it would be *terrible !* Terrible for us both."

There was a strange tone in the way he used this word, as if the thought *was* terrible to him.

It was the longest of nights. These words of his father *had* made some impression, and he saw there was truth in them. So, with a sort of spasmodic exertion, he really "made up leeway," as it is called, and strove to mend his fault of the night before; and thus was laying up fresh troubles and anguish for himself.

When the ladies were gone, there were the men in the smoking-room, the noisy chatter; and the Duke himself, who was in a chatty humour, attached himself to Charles.

"Yes, we shall have you at Banff. We leave this the day after to-morrow, and I have just settled with your father you must come with us."

"Go with you!" The young man gave a start. "Now?"

"It will be no inconvenience, I assure you. I should like to have you with us, and Lady Rosa will like it too. And you must stay a long time. I can give you capital deer-stalking and shooting."

"It is so kind of you," the young man murmured; "but I know it will put you out. Besides, I have preparations—"

The Duke laughed.

"A young man—preparations! Oh, very good. Not ball-dresses, wreaths, or flowers?

Ah! no; we can understand young ladies, and their great black boxes, which take days to get ready. No scruples, my dear fellow. We shall be a little in the rough, and I shall expect no ceremony."

At last, at about two o'clock, he had got rid of them, and got away to his own room, where he could be alone and think. Joy, rapture! On the table there was a tiny note, directed in a lady's hand. He flung himself on it, opened, and read—

"DEAR MR. BENBOW,

"Your letter made me happy. Such testimonials are always welcome, and encourage. I should be very glad to see you any time you would like to call, and should be glad to hear you *tell me those things*. Yes, you pity me with Mr. Hulkes. I knew you would. But this is one of the incidents of the profession. If we had no more than *that* to suffer! But I am getting accustomed to it all. But have you thought of this?—your family can hardly approve of you so *honouring a mere actress*. Certainly not your father. Believe me, it is better to look on from the boxes, and think of me only as Pauline. That distance lends such enchantment. Yes, come and see me, and admire me if you will—on the stage, and in my stage finery. Yours is not the only letter of praise I have received. I have two before me now, and set them side by side: one is that of a gentleman, the other that of a vulgarian. This last, *another* of our trials.—Always yours,

"LYDIA EFFINGHAM."

This threw him into an ecstasy. It was the most *piquant*, charming letter — nothing low, everything not only ladylike—(a poor compliment, after all, for "ladylike" stands for a dead level, conventional thing)—but it was womanly, heroic, noble, and like Pauline. And how full of a proper reserve! How charming that! He knew the dastardly rascal that was troubling her—the low, vulgar scoundrel that was thrusting his attentions on her, and with the lowest motives.

That gave him a sacred trust; he was bound to shield and protect her—a dear, interesting, divine creature, who had no protector. It was enough bliss for that night. Within the four corners of the page he could see a small, glittering view of the play—that blissful night: the look of the writing brought the whole scene before him. He could kiss its delicate characters several times over; he could lay it tenderly on his dressing-table—on a sort of throne of honour.

He had the sweetest sleep and the most delightful dreams. In short, he was "a boy in love," which means the 'Arabian Nights' Stories,' with all the treasures of enchantment, jewels, gold, silver, and beauty, laid open.

On the next day he must see her; he would brave all that dukes, fathers, or high-born girls would do to prevent him. He forgot all the difficulties in the way, the "persecution" that was likely to arise, and slept rapturously.

CHAPTER VIII.

LYDIA EFFINGHAM THE ACTRESS.

In the morning, what he thought persecution began. His father called him into the study—where, indeed, now actual meetings of the Vehmgericht seemed to be held.

" Well, you are going to the Duke. You will return engaged. I tell you so. But wait a day or so. See here, Charles," Mr. Benbow said, taking out his cheque-book, " we must spare no money on this expedition of yours. Take your man with you. I shall write to Pitt in London to send you down two of his best hunters—Lady Rosa admires good horsemanship. In fact, draw on me for what you like, and fill these two cheques for whatever is necessary. It is false economy, sparing anything on the last *coup*."

"But they are not going to-morrow, sir," he pleaded ; " we could get them to remain longer —such a short visit."

"I wish we could," said the other, abstractedly. " For somehow I fear you won't do much away from me. The Duke has business. But try yourself with her. Then it would only make the difference of a day or two."

" But must I go now, sir ? Is it not too sudden ? I have nothing ready. I don't see how it's to be done."

" But, my dear boy, you—a young fellow— don't want preparation—"

Encouraged by the good-natured tone, Charles came up to his father.

" You won't ask me to go—*at all* at present. You are always so kind. I shall make a botch of it, I know, and—"

" Sir ! "

There was a pause. The young man shrank away.

The father observed the effect, then said, quickly :

"You must go, sir. Send into the town and get what you want; and see, don't forget my warning of last night. And see, again: let me hear that all is settled finally within the three days. Go, sir."

Under this menace there was still a gleam of comfort, which Mr. Benbow did not know he was imparting—the expedition into Dipchester. There was a chance there, an age, a reprieve; though the execution might come to-morrow morning—execution, alas! from which there was no escaping.

So, after the usual spell of duty at lunch, and talking and attendance, he eagerly told Lady Rosa he must go and get some "things" —to be ready to set out with them in the morning, but would be back by dinner.

He had all but reassured that young lady, and this eagerness for departure helped to fortify the impression. She looked rather fondly on his handsome face.

He ran to his room to decorate himself, then

rushed to the stable for his horse, and in a moment was galloping into Dipchester.

Dipchester has its half-dozen show-houses of the old framed-house pattern, which hang over the pathway, with shops below, and little cottage-like windows. McCallum the draper's was one of these, and over McCallum's the new actress had lodgings. In such a place there is always repugnance to such a calling, attended with something like a holy horror. But Mr. McCallum had neat millinery young ladies— nice and pretty; and these soon made a party in favour of the beautiful lady up-stairs; who had none of the forward ways of the profession, but was interesting, polite, and ladylike, and asked up the Janes and Fannys to look at her dress when she was going out to do Pauline. McCallum, though a stern Scot, could not resist this popular feeling, and soon came round to her, and also to the steady respectable sheep-dog who guarded her (Miss Grant), and who had teeth to bite, and who *would* bite a Scotch-man too, if necessary. And very soon Mr.

McCallum, wife, family, and children, were seen in the boxes applauding with delight—which was not wonderful, considering that the admission tickets were "orders."

When Charles rode up to the door of the draper's shop and asked for Miss Effingham, great interest was exhibited among the young ladies of that house—to whom, indeed, he was known, having often purchased gloves, &c., there, by which patronage he conferred much honour. Miss Effingham was out; but one of the young ladies, who admired the gallant youth secretly, told him that the actress had gone for a walk across the fields, and had taken "her part" with her. The direction was described to him, and, after some hesitation, he set out and followed.

About Dipchester were all sorts of pleasant lanes and turnings—short cuts with stiles—that ran past plantations, and were really inviting. He was fond of the country; but on this day it seemed to him more inviting than ever it did —in fact, was it not *her* empire and dominion?

He had left his horse at the inn and wandered on, with a secret conviction—it seemed inspiration—that he would overtake her. Very soon he did : at least he saw a lady coming along swiftly, and attended, it would seem, by a gentleman—an apparition that made his cheeks flush, and the blood rush back to his heart. Who could this man be ? He stopped to watch, and then noticed that she was in front, walking very fast, and that there was some sort of dramatic action going on. Impelled by a sort of fate, he hurried to meet her. Then she cried, tremulously, "Oh, Mr. Benbow, I am so glad—*you* will protect me !"

He saw it was Mr. Hunter, the manufacturer —who was much discomposed at his arrival.

" Protect you," said the young man ; " who has dared—has this fellow—"

" Oh, come, I say, none of that," said Mr. Hunter. " There's no harm—what's all this fuss ? It's all very fine ! There are lots of actresses who come here, and are only too glad to get any notice."

"You had better go away," said Charles; "you are not desired here; and for the future, too, if anything of this sort is repeated, you'll bring about something very unpleasant."

"Oh! what will you do, Mr. Benbow?" said the other, in a fury. "Do you threaten me? I'm as good as you. Who are you, I'd like to know, that give directions to me?"

"Never mind that," said the young man. "I only warn you; and, as I stand here, if you dare to annoy this young lady again with this persecution, you shall have a sound thrashing,! There."

Never did Miss Effingham seem so lovely to him. She was excited; and there was a charming flush in her cheeks from the excitement. He was "her preserver"—that new character the acting of which, though lasting but a few moments, is equal to an attachment of years.

"What are you threatening me for?" said Mr. Hunter, in an insolent way. "What are you talking about thrashing, and that sort of thing? Miss Effingham didn't ask you to be her policeman and bully, did she? How dare you talk of thrashing, and that sort of thing, to me?"

"You had better give over all this, and go your own way, and let us go ours."

"I sha'n't. Who are you, and your lot, and your Dooks, up there? You're all *gentlemen*, I suppose. We've put up with too much—far too much of all your airs—from you and your set up there. I can tell you they're all sick of it about here, and it won't be stood much longer. There are better men about who could buy and sell every one of you and them."

"No doubt," said the other. "That is quite another question. But I tell you distinctly, your buying and selling notions won't do in this case. So, for the future, take warning."

"I intreat you, Mr. Benbow," she said, in the sweetest tones, "to let the matter be. This person, I am sure, will not trouble me any more."

"He had better not," said the young man, excitedly.

"Do you suppose I'll put up with this?" said

Mr. Hunter, quite furious at this contempt. "The road is open to me, and I'll walk on it; and I sha'n't go away at your bidding, nor at any one else's. This lady don't want you either. What damned work it is!"

And, putting his arms a-kimbo, he planted himself on the other side of Miss Effingham.

In a moment he was on his back in a convenient ditch. The young man was a skilful boxer. They were walking on; and, before Mr. Hunter could struggle out, the pair had reached the high road.

Charles was now indeed her protector and champion. How happy—how triumphant. the feeling! *There* was a tie to unite them. He was quite agitated at the thought. She was grateful, profusely grateful. It was such a happy walk home. He trod upon air all the time, walking side by side with his enchantress.

"How fortunate I am," he said, over and over again. "This is the luckiest day! How fortunate that I came on to-day instead of yesterday. Something really impelled me. It looks like a providence that I should have been sent to save you from that fellow."

"Indeed, I want a protector. If you only knew the persecution I have to endure from him. He tries to get into the house. He pursues me at the theatre. I cannot endure it."

"It will be different now," he said, eagerly. "I shall take care he never troubles you any more, and if he does——"

He stopped. He suddenly recollected that he could not remain, and must go to-morrow.

"Oh, but what shall I do! What am I saying and promising?" he exclaimed. "I have to go from this. You must be left here unprotected. Oh, it cannot be—it must not be!"

He then told her how his father required him to go on this visit. Forced him, in fact. He had done everything in his power. He would give the world to stay. She listened eagerly.

"It cannot be helped," she said; "I must only bear my lot—the actress's lot. We have no privilege, no protection, once we exhibit ourselves on the public stage.   That takes us out of the rank of ladies.   Yet I was born and brought up a lady!   No; I must only bear my lot like the rest.   This man will, of course, continue his persecution—nay, will revenge himself on me for what you have made him suffer.   But I must bear it."

They were now at her house.   The young man was in a strange state of doubt and distress. He knew not what to do for this noble young creature, brought to such distress.   And a lady, too!   How delighted he was to hear that news.   He could fling it in the teeth of those who slandered her.   For her he could be well content — and proud, too — to brave them all.

"So your father wishes you to go," she said, as they entered.   "Has he any special reason for this expedient?"

"Oh, of course he has some plans—some miserable plans that I am to carry out—a wretched mercenary marriage: to sell myself, in short, to buy rank and influence."

" And why should you not do this ? " she said, calmly. " It is a prudent thing, and what we are all taught to do by our parents."

" Pauline would not say that," he said, bitterly ; " but that is only in a play, of course. You do not care one way or the other. I suppose you have so much indulged in these imitative emotions that you have grown tired of all sentiment."

They were now up-stairs in the little modest apartments over McCallum's. There he found seated the elderly lady who seemed to be eternally knitting—Miss Grant, her aunt—and who, it was known, always attended her like a mother. It was a very happy evening for him. Tea was poured out for him by those enchanted fingers ; and, gradually, she gave him scraps and hints of her history—how she had been, as it were, forced on to the stage ; her father had died and left them all in distress ; and then she had felt it her duty to turn her talents to some profit. Thank God, she had helped them a great deal ; her poor talents had brought in something—at least, more than the miserable alms a governess receives.

"Going on the stage ! Mr. Benbow," she went on, like an inspired Corinna; "I know what is thought of that. What eyelids are raised! What shoulders shrugged ! It is a noble profession, if you have genius and brilliancy, and feel that you can move the crowd. Oh ! what I pine for is the great audience, the grand theatre, the thousand and one faces all turned towards the amphitheatre of intelligence, converging, like rays, to *you* as the centre ; the playing upon that vast and noble instrument ; the extracting of the faintest and most delicate tones, up to a crash loud as that of an organ ; the making them thrill and flutter ; then the turning them wild and delirious all at once, as if you were touching keys—what is there on earth approaching this ? From a child this dream has always been before me. And London ! LONDON ! Shall it ever be realized ?"

He looked at her with admiration. She seemed inspired.

"Whatever I can do—" he said, eagerly. "We have friends—influential friends—in town —that is," he added, hesitating, "my father has."

"Ah, I know," she said, gently. "I understand all that. He wishes you to get on—is ambitious. Even if he knew that at this moment you were wasting your time with a poor actress, instead of waiting on the great lady who *despises* me, who feels more contempt for me than she would for her maid—yet I am a lady, too, as I would prove to you; and my poor murdered father was a gentleman."

He started.

"Murdered."

"Not with knife or poison. There are other ways of murdering just as villainous. Never mind. Well, you are going on this visit, and you will know other actresses, and be as rapturous over them."

"No, never," he said. "I am not a child that they can send to school and order about. No, I must wait *now;* for that fellow would say

I fled from him. You must have some one to protect you, and it would be my glory to do so. Yes, I shall remain."

"What! and bring you into a quarrel with your father! Never! At least, not for me. I shall never see you again if you do. No one shall suffer for me."

"You cannot hinder it. Where you are, Miss Effingham, I shall be."

"Then you will drive me out of this place. I shall bring no one into trouble. I have enough trouble of my own on my head. No, you must go. *Why should you stay ?* "

"Because I love—I adore you !"

CHAPTER IX.

LOVE.

THE companion had left the room a little time before. She was not to hear this passionate declaration.

The actress started; then an expression of exquisite and tender sympathy—so it seemed to the adorer—came into her face; a sort of pity.

"What is this? what do you mean, my only poor boy? Do you know what you are saying, or going to do?"

"I am prepared for anything," he said. "I would face them all—face the world!"

"Marry an actress! You! They would think you would disgrace them."

"Marry a lady—a peerless lady—fit to place beside queens! I shall not rise till you consent."

"It would be the most cruel folly in the world did I do so. You do not know—you cannot see the difficulties. It is hopeless. You would only be sorry for it later."

"Never—never! I am yours—yours always, till death. If you do not consent, I shall go back, and before them all renounce all their plans publicly—then my father will turn me out of doors, and I shall be ruined: be ruined without you!"

She paused, and thought a moment. A curious look of triumph came into her eyes. It disturbed him.

"I am thinking," she said, in answer to his look, "what a glorious compliment this love of yours is to me. It is worth the applause of that great house which is my dream. It is the first gleam of sunshine I have had for years. I am proud of it. Indeed I am. After all, why should I punish you, or make you wretched? There is a fate in these things; and—let me confess this much to you—I *do* like you. Stay! But—but—this is all too hurried. I must make conditions."

He was in a rapture—in a tumult of gratitude. But she stopped him.

"Listen, and sit down calmly beside me while I speak. Think of me, if you like, as Pauline, and of yourself as Claude."

"As *your* Claude."

"Hush! This is only the second time you have seen me. Now, you must wait, and promise me to wait patiently. Indeed, I am serious in this—I must protect you. And, if you are advised by me, and are patient, I may promise that, after a time—"

He would agree to anything, if only *she* promised.

"You must stay here."

"That is fixed as fate. Only help me to do it. I am so inexperienced, and my father knows so much more. Your surpassing cleverness will show me how."

"There is only one way that I see. Go to

the Duke; tell him you have had a quarrel with this man; and that, as a gentleman, he will see how strange it would look your flying away. It seems a subterfuge; but I think of your interest."

What an inspiration! how clever! It seemed ever brilliant. It would have been years before he could have thought of it.

"It will not be much gain," she went on; "but still it will give you three or four days, since that is what you desire. Meantime, you will think all this over. *Both* of us shall think it over, and you will have time to repent of what you have said to me."

"Oh, but you will promise now. I rely on it —it is the only thing that will keep me up. You will not go back of your word?"

"I never go back of anything," she said. "But you must wait: indeed, yes! I know more of the world than you—even the stage world has taught me something. We learn something from plays; for those who wrote them knew the world very well. This is all too sudden—far too sudden, my dear Mr. Charles;

and, for my own sake as well as yours, I make
conditions. How could I tell that I could like
you ?"

"Oh ! Miss Effingham," he exclaimed, in
despair, "do you wish to crush me altogether ?"

" We have only seen each other twice, recollect
that. You would despise me if I were won in a
moment—brought to your wrist by a single
invitation, as if I was a hawk. Hawk, yes ! I
know who would call me that. No ; I should
like to learn to like you, and to teach you to like
me. Violent and sudden affection never lasts.
At the same time, I own that I like you ; and
will not deny that it is nearly certain that I
shall come to love you."

What more could he desire ? It was eminently
complimentary. He was being dealt with as a
man.

" Now," she went on, " let us talk of something else. Will you come and see Mrs. Haller
to-morrow night ? No ; I had forgotten—you are
ordered away."

"Yes," he said, pettishly. "Oh, but I am to stay now."

"No, you must not—I cannot allow it. Recollect now you take orders from me. You envied the Claude of the other night—that terrible Hulkes; well, do you know who is to be my Stranger?—Mr. Haggerston!"

The young man almost groaned. "Awful!" he cried.

"And I am expected to play, to do grand things with such people. It is enough to chill all the poetry, the animation, the dramatic feeling in my heart of hearts. That vulgarian will vulgarize *me*. Oh, that I had some one of gentle blood, some one of refinement—then you would see me act, indeed."

"I should not like to see that," he cried, eagerly; "and yet I suppose it will come to it one of these days. Up in London there are such noble, handsome actors; yet I could not wish to see you with them, unless—Oh, I wish I could play with you!"

"I do, indeed, wish you could; and you

could do it, even this very night. Proficiency, even without training, would make itself felt. If you acted as you did to-day, as you have always acted during the time I have known you —not very long—you might win a reputation."

"I would give the world," he said, "to have that privilege. If you would teach me—let me sit at your feet—"

"What are we talking of?" she said, smiling. "Bringing young Mr. Benbow on the stage— that would be news! We are indeed planning out a new life."

When young Mr. Benbow returned home, he found the Duke in the library, reading the 'Times.' In a few minutes, a sudden idea occurred to him; he had taken that august person into confidence. The young man's love had given him, of a sudden, tact, earnestness, and a sort of winning persuasiveness. He related his adventure with Hunter. The great man listened with interest.

"A young girl of this place—and who is she ?"

Charles adroitly turned this inquiry aside by loud denunciation of the vulgarity, the coarseness of "that Hunter;" in which the other agreed.

"Oh, certainly, I see it," he said; "if you left with us, at once, it would be said that you showed the white feather. Oh, no; that would not do at all. Not that I think the low rascal will take any notice—he has had enough."

"But my father, Duke," said the young man, growing more artful with his success, "he must not know; and yet how are we to account for my not setting off with you? There is the difficulty."

"Leave that to me," said the other; "it will only make a difference of a day or two, and we shall spare you for that time."

In a short time Mr. Benbow came in. The great man took him aside. The Benbow forehead grew wrinkled and disturbed. What did this mean?

"We won't have him for a day or two yet,"

said the Duke; "we may have to stop in town, and he can then follow us on. I have settled it all with Rosa."

"Ah, yes!" said Mr. Benbow, eagerly, as if that arrangement were after his own heart; "nothing could be better; we can send him to you then."

But grave suspicion and troubles began to fill his soul. This idiotic boy had been at some of his tricks. He must see to it at once.

The young man was in overpowering spirits. He was flying about "on air." He was so happy. He had succeeded; and she—so wonderful, clever, brilliant—had directed him. It was like an inspiration. But his father had him by the arm.

"I want you. Charles, what is the meaning of this?"

"I thought, sir, the Duke told you."

"Where were you after lunch?"

"Out riding, sir."

"By yourself?"

"Yes, sir. I went into Dipchester to buy

things for the journey, as you agreed I was to do, sir. Really, I don't understand—I do all you tell me to do—"

Again this was her inspiration. She was teaching him, he felt, many things.

His father thought a moment. Then said, "No doubt; I dare say you may be right. But I hope, Charles, you will bear my words in mind, *for your own sake.*"

It was now about five o'clock. The sound of wheels was heard outside, and a servant came to say that Dr. Fearon, the Dipchester doctor, whose visits were very frequent when there was company at the Castle—liking to make connection, under the mask of professional attendance —was come. Mr. Benbow was impatient when he heard that the Doctor wished to see him.

"What does the man want? Tell him there is nobody sick in the house."

The servant was going with this communication, when he was called back.

"I suppose I must see him, or he will take offence."

Young Mr. Charles had hurried away to his duties, and was very *empressé* in attention to the fair object who was laid out for him. He could afford to be so. For he had now coined a sort of fiction for himself that she was deputy, or in the place of the other. It was to her, the absent one, he seemed to be paying all these attentions. He was full of spirits and vivacity, and seemed to be really making way with that cold, haughty dame. Love was furnishing him out with spirit, energy, wit, or goodwill, which makes up for much that is wanting. Nothing could be better than the way everything was going off. There is a Providence that shapes our ends—" when we are all in love."

As he was dressing for dinner, the door was opened suddenly, and his father rushed in, pale, his face contorted with anger.

" What is this ? " he said at once. " How *dare* you attempt to tell me falsehoods ! I have heard the whole thing. It is over the place, this low adventure. How dare you attempt to deceive me with these falsehoods ? "

"Falsehoods, father—that is a very strong word." She was giving him courage.

"Yes, falsehoods. I see your low contemptible game; and it has shocked me and made me ashamed. I tell you this solemnly, sir, on this spot—you shall pack off to-morrow, and with them!"

"Father, you mistake the whole thing. The Duke knows all. How could I help meeting Mr. Hunter, or avoid interfering?"

"Knows all! Another falsehood."

"Yes, all: I told him everything. I saw Miss Effingham coming across the fields, and this man pursuing her—persecuting her with his low attentions; and I did what any *gentleman* would have done—what you *must* have done yourself, father—gone up and protected her, and thrashed the fellow. The Duke says I would be showing the white feather and disgracing us all if I went off in the morning."

This was such a new strain for his son—the argument was so well put, and so forcible and reasonable in its tone—that the father was pleased in spite of himself. Love, wonderful love !—rhetorician as well !

"I don't care. It's most unlucky and unfortunate. I can only give you my old caution, Charles," he said. "Make what pretexts and ingenious excuses you like—indulge yourself in what fancies you please! but this matter must go on. Now, come down to dinner."

CHAPTER X.

THE Dipchester doctor was kept for dinner, according to the form in that case made and provided. It was an honour, and he was delighted that it had been paid to him. In the course of that banquet, however, he thought he could best recommend himself by bringing round the conversation, in a complimentary way, to the " fracash "—-so he styled it—which had taken place that morning.

" And, indeed," he said, " we are all glad of it down there; for that Hunter wanted taking down a bit—always bragging of this thing and the other, and of his money—of which he is close enough."

The Duke was listening. " And this young lady, Dr. Fearon," he asked, " who was she ? "

" Oh, the actress, my lord Duke, Miss Lydia Effingham—a fine handsome woman, that's turning half the young fellows' heads in the place. We can't blame Mr. Charles, after all."

" Indeed ! " said the Duke, with some astonishment, looking over at Charles. " You did not tell me that."

His companion turned to him with scorn.

" This is like a dramatic surprise out of one of their plays. We shall begin to understand it all by and by."

" It was merely an accident," said the young man, confused. " I was passing through the fields, and came upon the scene at the very moment. I could have made no *appointment*— you must see that."

" I really cannot say," replied the young lady haughtily ; " and I did not think so ; *qui s'excuse*, you know. I don't understand this sort of thing."

Women have much instinct in these matters, and that moment Lady Rosa was convinced of what she had before suspected, even so early

as the incident of the bouquet, that her young
admirer was false, was playing a part, and fascin-
ated by this actress. She turned from him
haughtily, and answered him in a cold dry
fashion for the rest of dinner. This Mr. Benbow
saw with something like anguish. It was a
miserable dinner for him, and all the fine baked
meats and juices were so much chewed ashes in
his mouth. He too had his mistrust that the
plan would somehow or another fail.

When the ladies went up, the doctor, feeling
that it was a point upon which he was very
strong, brought the subject back again.

" I don't think Hunter will take any notice.
I hear he says Mr. Charles is too young, and that
he would make himself ridiculous. But I must
say, my lord Duke, the actress is worth it in
every way—the finest woman you ever saw in
the whole course of your life."

" I have seen her—we have all seen her," said
the great man, with dignity. " But I can hardly
join in all that high commendation. Is she
drawing in your town ? "

"Oh, Haggerston is making money out of her; the place is half full every night."

"Half full! that can hardly pay," said one of the gentlemen.

"Lord bless you, sir, yes; it keeps all going, you know, when there's about twenty people scattered about the house. At least, there's little loss; but benefits and bespeaks bring it up. She's to have one."

"How long," asked Mr. Benbow, abruptly, "does this engagement go on?"

"Oh, as long as it pays, Mr. Benbow, Mr. Haggerston told me; and he means to work her out so long as there's a sixpence in her." The doctor was a very awkward gentleman, as it has been seen.

"She's coming out in Mrs. Haller to-morrow night, with Haggerston as the Stranger," cried the young man, forgetful of everything in his eagerness. "She will play it superbly. You know the story, Duke. I can see her pathetic face now as the poor woman deserted by her husband. We might all go again. It would be well worth it. Only fancy! It seems like a sacrilege to have to play with a ruffian of that sort! Why, it will be a burlesque, and chill every feeling of poetry and sentiment in her. How can she be expected to throw herself into the part, with a coarse fellow of that kind before her? How can—"

"No more wine, Duke?" said his father, abruptly; "then we may join the ladies."

Strange to say there was no interview that night between father and son.

CHAPTER XI.

THE next morning the august ducal party went away, in solemn state. Great benefactions were distributed, almost regal in their magnificence; and the exact figure was known in Dipchester before the day was over. Mr. Benbow was calm, and appeared satisfied.

"You must wait at home, Charles," he said, "in case that fellow should come out here to look after you. You are clever enough to deal with him, whatever purpose he may have in view. Fighting, of course, is laughable; especially with a fellow of that sort. If he is insolent, give him another thrashing and kick him out. In fact, if I were to advise, I would try and bring it to that. No man, by whatever bluster, could get over a double beating. I am driving to the agent's house, to look over the books."

This was delightful: this absence was certain for three or four hours. He could seize the opportunity; but then, something whispered to him, like Sir Lucius, "Your honour, your honour!" He was a gentleman, and certainly not inclined to sacrifice the credit of his family. Better still, should he not wait until evening? when he must see the divine Haller or die—*i. e.* be miserable.

He waited in, therefore, all the morning; but Mr. Hunter never came. He was, then, going to take no notice. Young Benbow was a mere boy, and beneath his contempt. He was not going to get into a quarrel about a mere strolling actress. And so the nine hours' wonder dropped there. But it was a long, weary, dragging time.

This he was not entitled to assume was the real reason. Mr. Benbow had actually driven to his factory and called on him, and after an interview, which was of a good-humoured sort, from the loud laughter that came from the room, retired, having made all up in a light way.

"He is a foolish boy," said Mr. Benbow, "and should not attempt to interfere with you and your actress, whom you think of as a man of the world should."

"A regular schemer, Mr. Benbow," said the manufacturer.

"Exactly what I set her down for," said Mr. Benbow.

It was settled that Mr. Hunter should come and dine shortly, and Mr. Benbow left him much gratified by the visit.

In the afternoon Mr. Benbow senior returned —his face smooth, his air calm and cheerful, though the agent's books, &c., had not been very satisfactory. Money would have to be got in the market to defray the heavy cost of the recent entertainment. It was screwing and pinching, and fresh encumbrances; and it was wonderful he was not anxious. But it was so much money on zero. That figure would surely turn up : he had covered it again and again. Only wait : it was coming now.

Towards night, Mr. Benbow—who, when alone, often ate his meal standing—partook of a frugal repast. After he had snatched a few scraps he withdrew into his own study, where, with his arms out, he plunged into the angry billows of papers and business. It seemed a little curious that he should exercise no jealous watch over his son, who was not a little surprised at this indifference, and who, leaving word that he was "gone out for a stroll," set off with exultation, and in full dress for Dipchester.

As he got to the town, the sight of the coarsely-done posters with—" Renewed Triumph ! Great Success ! First Night of 'Guilty Love and Christian Forgiveness ; or, the Stranger '"— country managers are fond of thus intensifying the titles of too familiar plays—made his heart flutter. A great band of red letters, looking like a belt of gore, told the world that Mrs. Haller was to be sustained by the "unique" actress, Miss Lydia Effingham ; while Mr. Haggerston, for this night only, would give his great impersonation of the Stranger. He hurried on, fearful of being late; reached the little, old-fashioned house, which, though lit up, to his wonder and indignation, had a sort of illuminated desertion.

He entered. It was a very thin house indeed.

Five or six people in the boxes, a dozen or so in the pit, and what seemed scattered videttes all through the galleries. A kind of solemn, cavernous declamation was travelling through the house; and Charles saw a stout gentleman, in a high-collared green frock coat, with cape and brass buttons and hunting-boots, sitting down on a long box covered with green cloth, and indulging in his sorrows. Mr. Haggerston seemed to address his remarks with equal impartiality to different persons in the house, and took note of Mr. Charles Benbow as he entered. The latter paid him the courtesy of sitting down for a few seconds and listening; and, looking round the house, saw that Mr. Hunter was also present, in a box close to the stage. Charles presently rose, full of impatience to be with her whom he so passionately loved, and who, from Mr. Haggerston's remarks, was not to appear for some time. He went round and tapped at the door in the box-lobby, which led on to the stage. It was opened by a villager, the same who wore Mr. Haggerston's state livery on that famous occasion of a "command night."

"All right," said Mr. Charles, with a smile, and advanced; but the door was kept nearly closed.

"Can't come in, sir. No one admitted behind the scenes."

"Rubbish!" said Charles, angrily. "You know me—there, let me pass."

"Can't indeed, sir; I'm very sorry—against the rule."

"I'll complain of you to Mr. Haggerston, and get you punished for your impertinence. Go and tell him that I am here."

"It's 'is hown horders," said the villager, heedlessly, or from agitation, multiplying his *h*'s.

"His orders! nonsense! Here—" and the

usual convincing syllogism in the shape of half-a-crown was laid down.

"Indeed, sir," said the man, in a low voice, answering the call, "he said particular I wasn't to let *you* pass. But he is off now, and you can speak to him yourself, sir."

"What's this?" said the Stranger, roughly; "who is this trying to force their way behind my scenes?"

"Mr. Haggerston, is this impertinence directed by you? What is over you to-night?"

The manager, in his green coat and boots, stood in the doorway.

"Young sir," he said, "I can't have it, and it can't be. The regulations of my theatre must be enforced. That is to say—ah, how d'ye do, Mr. Hunter?"

That gentleman was behind, listening with an engaging smile.

"I wanted to speak to you, Haggerston," he said.

"Certainly, Mr. Hunter, if you have business with me; but I can't turn my ' 'hind scenes ' into a lounge for all the idle young men of the place."

"Let me pass at once," said Mr. Benbow; "turn me out if you dare. I wish to speak to Miss Effingham. Lay your hand on me, one of you! I gave this gentleman a lesson yesterday."

There was something in his manner, as well as in this reminder, which had its effect. He pushed by them both, and was beside the lovely Mrs. Haller in a moment, pouring out his complaint.

"The man is mad," he said. "What can be the meaning of this insolence? I suppose he wants to take part with that low Hunter."

"I can explain it," she said, more simply. "It is directed against me. *Your father was with him to-day.*"

"I see. The venal wretch has been bought. Never mind, we can despise him."

"He has been strange in his behaviour to me also, and—"

"What! has he dared—"

Mr. Haggerston was now before them.

"Now see here. This won't do at all, Mr. Benbow. I don't, of course, want to make confusion ' 'hind scenes ' "—a favourite word of his—"by turning you out; but, understand, I won't have it again. And you, too, Miss Effingham; I trust *you'll* conform to the regulations, and not be encouraging all the young men of the place to come here. The engagement is not so profitable to me as to entitle you to take such liberties."

"You fellow, don't dare to speak to this lady in that style, or I'll give you a lesson—"

"Take care, you, sir," said Mr. Haggerston, clapping his hand on his stage sword. "No bullying to me, sir. Raise your hand to me, and I'll have in the police."

"Hush," said Miss Effingham, "I see what all this means, and will simplify the matter immensely. I know the whole reason of your behaviour to me and to this gentleman, and can save you a great deal of trouble. You wish to end my engagement."

"I don't say that, ma'am. It has turned out most unremunerative to me, but—"

"Then we *shall* end it. When you please. Now—on the spot. Give out after the play that it is the last night of the engagement."

"Oh, that will hardly settle it," he said; "I ought to have some indemnity for what I have lost by it. But you are too hasty, Miss Effingham. I don't mean to go quite so far as that." There's your ben. yet, and my ben. Oh no, I won't be taken so short as that."

"But I do. He is afraid," she said, with a smile, to her lover, "that those who set him on in this matter may not be so liberal in their intentions as to cover all loss in the affair."

"Leave all that to me," said the young man, eagerly. "I am witness. I heard him agree to it—indeed, he proposed it."

Mr. Haggerston was furious. But the audience were growing impatient, and the Stranger and Mrs. Haller had to go on. Charles went into the boxes, and looked on, enraptured. He thought she never played so magnificently, and

that she was playing to him. Perhaps she was.
It was all only too short, and he was grieved
when the play was done.

He walked home with her—her friend keeping close to them. He told her that this now
brought matters to a crisis, and he was not
sorry for it. "It is I," he said, "who am the
cause of this. Not only honour, but simple
justice, require that I should stand by you.
There is no compliment in the matter. I am
yours for ever and ever. We must look the
thing in the face: difficulties are gradually
encompassing us; and this night settles our
destiny. You must decide—oh, you must!
You are thrown on the world. It is idle
opposing me; for I shall follow you wherever
you go, even if I ruin myself with my father.
Better now make me some promise—agree that
you will be mine; and then I shall agree to
obey you in everything, and be guided by you
in everything."

She paused, and thought a moment.

"I have wished to save you from this, but it

is not my doing. Your father has hurried on
whatever is to happen now. You must at
least consent to a few days' interval. Recollect
this is the *third* time you have seen me, and
you want me to be yours for *eternity*. I must
think—ponder it over, before a decision. You
would despise me yourself if I took any important step without deliberation. In the
morning I shall tell you."

"No, no, no! I may be going in the morning, and I must know now."

She shook her head.

"Come here, then, before you go, and then
you will learn my final determination. You
will grant me this little delay, will you not?
It is for your good—all for your good. Indeed
it is. I like you too well to let you ruin yourself; and, if we must yield to the inevitable,
let it be borne without mischief if we can."

"I care not what may happen so that I shall
win you !"

"Ah, you little know—you have not been
tried yet. Once let your father *really* exert

himself in this matter, and you will find yourself weak before him. You know you will.
You cannot deny it. He is not alive yet to
the danger; but, if he were to set himself
seriously to *crush* you—you without means,
money, power—what *could* you do then?"

Her foolish boy looked a little scared at this
picture.

"Crush me! But he would not. He likes
me. When he sees my heart is set on this
matter, I know—I am sure—he will give way."

"What! and allow you to marry an actress
instead of a duke's daughter! Ah, you know
it will be hard to resist him. Never mind; we
shall see in time. You shall know it all from
me in the morning."

CHAPTER XII.

But in the morning the young man had to set off, equipped, money in his purse, and more promises for the future.

His father was very kind, and he was touched by the kindness; so much so that he felt not a little ashamed of his selfishness.

" I have been a little harsh and peremptory to you of late," he said, " but I have been sadly worried. It is hard to find a favourite scheme not going well. This little *penchant* of yours is well enough for amusement; but business is business. I must tell you, you have, so far, behaved in a rather unmanly and ungentlemanly way to Lady Rosa. Her rank and the Duke's should have protected her from being played fast and loose with in this way."

" I did not mean it, indeed," said the young man, rather shocked at this new view.

" Well, you must really make up for it—I insist on it—and do away with the impression. It is a mortifying position for a young person of such rank, especially, to hear you openly puffing a common peripatetic creature—at thirty shillings a week. However, to leave it to your good sense and honour, at least, remove the bad impression."

" After all," he thought, " there was no hurry. It might never come to anything." Meanwhile he could be rapturously happy for the time; never looking forwards or backwards; giving himself up to the exquisite dream; and reckless of the consequences. He was driven in a dog-cart; and, when he got to Dipchester, he stopped at the inn, and walked away to see her who was now his all.

As he walked through the town he passed by a flaming orange poster, which was headed by the words which to him had the look of a talisman—the chime of the most exquisite music —" Theatre Royal, Dipchester;" and, feeling his very heart stirred, he stopped to read. He was filled with fury and amazement as he read—

THEATRE ROYAL, DIPCHESTER.

Mr. Haggerston, while returning thanks to his patrons for their ever generous support, and while wishing to merit future favours by an unflagging zeal, begs to inform them that, as MISS LYDIA EFFINGHAM, with whom a costly engagement had been effected, has chosen, in an abrupt and unwarrantable way, to terminate her engagement, he has been compelled to secure, at a moment's notice and enormous expense, other talent; and has succeeded in catering for his friends the services of that eminent tragedienne,

MRS. HECTOR MANFRONE,

Who will make her first appearance in

THE MURDERER'S DAUGHTER.

Anne Redman (the murderer's daughter) MRS. HECTOR MANFRONE.
John Redman (the murderer)   .   Mr. Haggerston.

He was furious at this scandalous libel. The bill was still damp, and he indignantly tore it down and trampled it under foot to the astonishment of some Dipchestrians. He then hurried away to the draper's shop. The young lady at the shop who so admired him came to meet him.

" Oh, she is gone, sir ! "

" Gone ! Where ? When ? What does this mean ? "

" I don't know, I'm sure, sir. She left this note for you."

And one was handed to him, which he tore open and read :

" Thinking of your interest more than my own, I have thought it best to save you from a storm and a persecution which it would be cruel to ask you to face. I own to you that this is my reason, and this alone. You have not seen the world ; you know not your own strength or weakness. The whole would end disastrously for us both. Should I be induced to invest all my love, my affections, in one whom I *do* like and admire, I might find myself deserted ; and there, where ' I have garnered up my heart,' as they say in one of the plays, I would find a snare and unsubstantial support—not being able to trust myself or to trust you. Do not be angry. I have resolved to fly and hide myself. You will not find me, so do not try. I would not entail misery on you for the world. You would be persecuted to death. As I told you before, if you are constant, and, after a lapse of time, feel that you cannot live without me, perhaps—but it is right that you should know this, and I give it by way of warning: it will be better for you to have *nothing to do with me*. My life has another purpose than to be devoted to all that is loving or affectionate. *To that purpose I am bound to sacrifice everything—nay, to turn everything;* and, if that purpose required it, I should have to sacrifice one I loved. Accept these words of warning, indeed extorted from me. They will make you hate me; but that would be better than your ruin. Do not try and find me. You will, of course, if you try; for by love I know all difficulties are overcome. But I had rather that you should forget me.

" LYDIA EFFINGHAM.

" Think of this, too. What do you know of me—or who I may be? Whether this be my real name or no? Think of all these things, and see how hopeless the matter becomes, and how much better it is that it should end here for ever."

He read this with a despair and wonder mixed. The arguments in it, as might be expected, had not the least effect on his mind—the appeal it contained not the least weight.   It is strange how, with some minds, always a different conclusion is drawn to that which is intended.

The milliner's girl read in his agitated face the whole story, and understood it as well as if it had been told to her.

It was not very difficult for the distracted youth to discover her track.   It seemed to him that he was a miracle of cleverness when he bethought him of asking at the railway what special ticket she had taken.   The clerk, one of histrionic tastes, was able to tell him.   It was a through ticket for one of the great manufacturing towns.   It would take her the whole day to get there.   Something could be done by telegraphing.

His father knew an important person in that

place ; and to the son of this gentleman he telegraphed, begging him to watch the motions of a person who would arrive by that train.

All thought of the Duke and the Duke's daughter ; all thought of his father's brilliant plans and hopes—those anxious dreams which the son well knew, at that very moment, were wearing away the father's brain, and very heart —all were forgotten in this infatuation ; and, in a few minutes, he was seated in a train that took another direction to the one which was to have brought him to the palace of enchantment, of dazzling hopes, of wealth, of power, and happiness.

CHAPTER XIII.

DISAPPOINTED.

Mr. Benbow, when his son had left him, had a light heart and a smoother brow. He became complaisant. The visit, he had settled, should last a fortnight; but the great potentate had made a significant speech, as he shook hands with his host:

"It, indeed, rests with himself how long he shall stay with us."

Not that Mr. Benbow was wholly reassured. His confidence in the sense of his son had been greatly shaken. He was, indeed, a little scared. For the young fellow had never been put to such a test before: had always seemed a sort of humdrum, average, *guidable* disposition, which, if it could not lead, could at least be led; now he was changed.

All this was alarming. Still, so far he had made all sure ; and all would go well. He went into Dipchester at his leisure, and contrived to meet Mr. Haggerston. That manager was exuberantly obsequious.

"I think we managed well, sir—dissolved the engagement at a heavy sacrifice to me ; a *very* heavy sacrifice ; but we have saved your son from the siren "

"I hear you had a succession of bad houses," the other said, coolly. "I am sorry to learn it ; but shall not forget what you have done, Mr. Haggerston."

"Yes, sir, we drove her out of the town—regularly routed her."

"What, has she gone ? "

And Mr. Benbow started. He thought there was some indistinct symptom of danger in *both* going on a journey at the same time. Could there be any relation between these two movements ?

Still, she was gone. She was out of his path —a poor strolling actress, obliged to earn her "bit and sup"—nothing more or less than a scheming adventuress.

He knew boys well. The dazzling attractions of the Duke's " palace ; " the charming girls ; the attentions, and even flattery, which his son would meet with from some ; above all, the Duke's daughter tendered for his acceptance ; the state, the magnificence of Banff Castle—all this he knew quite well. He himself had been love-sick once in his boyhood, when he had been passionately attached—he was ashamed as he thought of it—to a curate's daughter. Ah ! the pang ! A curate's daughter ! A prudent father, bless him for it, had behaved with stern cruelty —torn him from her savagely. It had been the blessing of his life. Where would he have been at that moment only for that ?

Altogether he was content, and went home happy. *En attendant*, he busied himself with minor plots and schemes, which filled up his mind.

Thus two days went by, and a third day and a fourth ; when he began to wonder that he had not received an account of the progress made. But he knew his son well. The lad had no business habits; answered letters fitfully; and scarcely ever volunteered them. Two days more had passed; then an entire week.

This silence actually gave him hope. Everything had been settled, and would burst on him with all the suddenness of completion. But then another week began to glide by; and, finally, on one morning he received a letter with the Duke's name outside, in the corner. It contained the following astounding news:

"DEAR BENBOW,

"We have been expecting your son every day. I suppose we need not expect him further. His room has been waiting for him all this time. Still, it is strange that neither he nor you should have written. Pray let us have a line to explain this singular delay, and believe me, yours sincerely,

"BANFFSHIRE."

Mr. Benbow tottered—in fact, was nearer a stroke than ever he was in the whole course of his life. All he could gasp out was, "The scoundrel—the low, hypocritical scoundrel!—where is here? where is he?" No one could answer him this. He could utter no other question, for his voice was failing him; but he was answered by another letter, which he saw lying on the table before him, and on which he pounced. He tore it open. It ran:

"MY DEAR FATHER,

"You will be surprised to hear that I have not been at the Duke's after all; but I must tell you that important reasons may prevent me going to him—reasons which I know your good sense, kindness, and generosity will approve. I think it would be idle to enter on them now; more idle to present myself at Banff at all. I have thought the matter deeply over; and, after calm deliberation, have come to the resolution that it would be dishonourable to introduce myself into a house, or try and win the affections of a young lady to whom I could offer none in return. I scorn to do so; and I beg you will not ask me.

"Under these circumstances I have not been able to summon courage to go on with my journey; and submit to your better judgment if it would not be more for our advantage to think no more of the plan. Waiting your commands, I am, my dear father, your affectionate son."

He fell back speechless; crushed with disappointment—despair, rather—and rage. But his character had always been of the sort that rises with an emergency. In a moment he was coolly considering what was the next rigorous step he should take.

This fool, this child — infant, rather—who should be treated as such. Never mind; he who had never been baffled by strong men—men of intellect and genius,—should not be opposed by a poor creature of that sort. Before an hour was out he had determined on his plans; and before the expiration of two hours he was on his road to that far-off manufacturing town from which his son had written.

CHAPTER XIV.

A HEROINE.

LEAVING Mr. Benbow in his trouble we will shift the scene to the Ducal district at St. Arthur's-on-the-Sea, where much festivity was about to set in.

St. Arthur's-on the-Sea was a bathing town combined with a packet station: and a harbour that, to any one looking from the inland hills, seemed like a loop of delicate ribbon floating on the water. It was a granite district, and the abundance of plaster, frosting over villas as though they were bride-cakes, made the place glitter and shine in the glare of the sun, like an Italian bay.

It was also a yachting station, and two clubs, the Royal St. Arthur's, and the Royal Burgee, frowned and scowled at each other from opposite sides of the jetty. The St. Arthur's was select, and, though founded on a broad platform, by-and-bye began to black-ball various local persons as "low" and "not the sort of person." But the famous rejection of Mr. Littlejohn, the solicitor, whom every one knew, and whom many of the "fine" party—men, for instance, like Foljambe and Knox, ruthless "beaners"—were willing to admit, brought matters to a crisis. Then it was determined to found the Royal Burgee.

Once every year a regatta was given by both clubs, conjointly—an act, however, in which there was no amity or cordiality. It was imposed by sheer necessity, as neither could have separately borne the cost of entertaining. They gave plates and prizes together; but somehow the St. Arthur's contrived to bear off any honour or profit that was to be got out of the strangers of rank, much as a lady of condition will ignore the client to whose party she has undertaken to ask guests. The distinguished strangers always chose the St. Arthur's, when offered honorary membership. They were "put up" to the matter almost before they touched shore by the Reverend Doctor Bailey, who was for "keeping the club pure, sir," and threw out, in a careless parenthesis, that "the other place" was "a kind of poor thing, you know," mostly "brokers and the shopkeepers," well-conducted and respectable, and all that; but scarcely the sort of thing. "And it is gratifying for me," continued the doctor, a very enormous clergyman, six feet two in height, and portly and weighty without absolute corpulence, "to see persons of that class, banding themselves together for rational relaxation. If they want their club, why shouldn't they *have* it? and Heaven speed their work; and I am told it is exceedingly well-conducted, but it is scarcely the place, you see. You are a man of the world, Sir John."

The Reverend Doctor Bailey, thus mentioned, was the recently-appointed vicar of this important and fast-rising watering-place. In appearance, he was a very remarkable-looking man of great height; he had a vast broad chest; a flourishing umbrella; a broad-brimmed hat, and an unhealthy florid face; lips that were made for sauces and wines; with a high stiff wall of a white tie, which came up at the side of his neck, and seemed bent on cutting off his ears. The hat lay very far back, and the Reverend Doctor Bailey, stalking along, his head back, his "snub" nose to the clouds, was as well-known an object as the spire of the church he served. That church, with a wise forethought, he had accepted when the place was a poor one. With a true instinct as to its future, he had asked his patron, Lord Frogmore, for the living, and it had been worked up into a most profitable "berth." He was a good preacher, or had the reputation of being one, which did as well; and during the season the doctor contributed much to its success by his genteel sermons, in which there was none of that vulgar conventicle language, which he called mere "low poking the fire," and which he said fretted unnecessarily the nice and good people who came to hear him. "Not that

I would compromise the truth," he said, "one hair's-breadth. I shall do my sacred work always faithfully and to the best of my power: but the roaring vulgarity of such fellows as that Buckley, who has the little Bethel yonder, does no good."

There was a parsonage next the church, a very small apostolic mansion. Long ago it had been given over to the curate at a rent, while the doctor gave his dinner-parties up at the Beeches, a handsome gentleman's seat which he had purchased. There he lived with Mrs. Bailey, whose little shrunk figure no one was familiar with, with his daughter Jessica and his son Tom —a young fellow in the army, often spoken of as "the captain." These children had unhappily been born when Doctor Bailey was "a mere working curate," and had not yet established his connection; he often regretted that one had not been christened Constantia, after "dear Lady Frogmore," and the other St. John, a family name of the same house. Nay, turning his regrets still further back, the doctor would bewail his excessive haste in the matter of marriage, when he might have chosen something far more "suitable;" the truth being that Mrs. Bailey's origin would not bear heraldic tracing, nor was she even fortified with useful connection. But, with a venial exaggeration, if not untruth, the doctor devised conversational pedigrees, spoke of Mrs. Bailey's "family," and very largely of "the Bakers of Blackforest."

Thus much for allusion to the doctor, who was, as it were, viceroy of the place, and was really allowed to take on himself all representative duties. He was, indeed, described as an "overbearing, choleric, insolent fellow," by one of the radicals of the town, and, "a clerical bully," who, at home, roared at his family, though he was a little afraid of his daughter. A selfish schemer, with no more religion about him than was confined strictly to his Sunday platitudes. *Then*, it was owned, he shone, working his arms vigorously, and having a tremendous pair of lungs. Thus much for the doctor's house. But there is a family, whose heiress daughter is a heroine of this little piece, who must be noticed before the figures themselves enter from the wing.

Panton Park lay well back in the country, and the owner, Sir Charles Panton, a true squire and hunting man, boasted that the sea could not be seen from his top windows. Yet it was not more than a mile and a half from the bathing town, down in a rich bowl of grass and planting. There, in a great stone palace which the late owner had built fifty years before, literally not knowing what else to do with his money, lived Sir Charles and daughter. She was heiress— magic title of honour, that has made many hearts thrill more than the loveliest faces on this earth. More conjuring has been done with that spell than with any other, which brings with it beauty, grace, wit, honour, virtue, and accomplishment. And Miss Laura Panton was an heiress combining the blessings of fifteen thousand a year, with "savings," a park and mansion, with a town house in Brook-street, and, what was not the least of all in the eyes of matrons with young candidates, a father, grey, rather stricken in years, though wiry. Such rare attractions soon became well known, and indeed it was said that St. Arthur's-on-the-Sea owed as much to them as to its other natural advantages of fine air and bathing. But she was delicate; had a weak fragile chest, and, though small and refined-looking, with a well-bred haughty air, seemed bloodless, and was said once to have broken a blood-vessel in her throat. Hence she and her father had to pass each winter at one of those hiding-places where poor invalids run timorously from Boreas and Eurus. The gossips also said she was flighty and fanciful; gay, too gay, and, for all her delicacy, passionately fond of the world and its delights.

Sir Charles had been originally a Mr. Wright, a plain unassuming gentleman of very moderate means. He had sent his only child to a "finishing" school, where also the parson's daughter, Miss Bailey, had been placed by her father, not from any paternal anxiety to give her the best, that is, the most costly, education possible, but because it might lead to acquaintances, "nice connection, you know," for himself. How simple, having thus laid a foundation, to proceed in this way, with an engaging smile: "Not Mr. Dashwood, surely? Might I ask, any way connected with a charming young lady that was at Dampier House with my little girl? Wonderful! My dear sir, I am the clergyman here, &c." It was while this delicate Miss Wright, whose health was so precarious, was here, that the two girls first met.

The truth was, the school had accepted Jessica at a reduced premium, for a mere trifle: in fact, the doctor valuing his position and possible recommendations at the difference. *Their* view was that he would surely do them mischief, and injure the school, if they refused his terms. And it is certain the doctor would have steadily shrugged his shoulders, and pished and poohed the establishment into ruin. "A very poor sort of place, sir; all sorts of paw-paw people. A lucky escape of sending my girl there!" But the lady directors, true to the instincts of their kind, "took it out" of the unhappy little hostage thus confided to them, and they had instinct to see that from that indifferent father would come no protest. She was kept there for six years, going through the whole " curriculum," such as it was, and going through a course of steady mortification, bitter drudgery, with that hot iron of dependency which the Misses Proudfoot forced steadily, day by day, and hour by hour, to enter into her child's soul. The vicar's daughter could not be treated with open disrespect; but it was known to every one that the pale, and worn, and studious child was· " on charity," more or less. So pale and thoughtful she was now, having been slowly changed from the gay, romping, rosy-cheeked " little thing " which she had been when she arrived.

When the new girl, just come, " Wright," was known to be the daughter of a gentleman of slender means, the Misses Proudfoot had some reluctance about accepting her, owing to a possible uncertainty about the premiums. From parents of this undesirable sort the moneys had to be dug out, must be, as it were, crushed and broken up from quartz masses, collected in grains, after long delays, excuses, appeals, &c. But the references were genteel.   She was a curious girl — delicate, peevish, fretful, full of humours, ready to complain of her companions, and to turn away from the excellent fare provided for them.   She took as many airs as a bishop's niece whom they once instructed, and whom the bishop, an " honourable and reverend," came to see in full apron.   They hardly knew how to deal with her, for she seemed dangerous and vindictive, and could injure the school.

She had one friend among the girls, who clung to her with a romantic friendship and adoration.   This was the parson's daughter, who, from the moment of her arrival, had become her jackal and defender, her admirer and worshipper. It was inconceivable, the services she rendered, the devotion she paid.   She was more useful than an Eton fag, because her service was voluntary.   She shielded her from punishment when the other could not shield herself; she followed her with loving eyes, like a faithful dog; and when " Wright " (for the young ladies spoke of each other in this gentlemanly way) was sick, stole off to watch her, in defiance of the rules of the establishment. The determined breach of these laws brought a tart letter to the doctor, who came off in an angry fluster, blowing and puffing, and began to revile his child for her scandalous ingratitude for the blessings of a good education. " I am told you are going after low mean creatures, sticking to them with a disgusting familiarity, separating yourself from the nice young ladies of the establishment. Do you suppose, girl, I can pay for you here, stinting myself in common luxuries, all for you to follow your grovelling whims and these vulgar tastes? There are plenty of nice, well-connected girls in the house whose friendship would be useful, and useful to *me* too; and you choose to go puddling in the gutter, making dirt pies! Faugh! It's disgusting." The reproof had no effect, and the father even remarked, from the first, a cold insensible look in the eyes of his child, fruits of the excellent training he had been passing her through.

The young girl recovered, "joined her companions," more pettish and helpless than before, and was received with affectionate rapture by her faithful henchwoman. What was the secret of this singular devotion? Possibly there was none. It was her humour, or there was in the fretful eyes of the other girl a faint expression of suffering which drew her pity irresistibly. Sometimes a *look* of this sort has strong and permanent fascination. The other showed neither gratitude nor love; but Jessica was quite content.

CHAPTER XV.

THE BEGINNING OF THE VENDETTA.

Suddenly, one fine morning, there was a flutter and bustle at Dampier House, and it was known that strangers had arrived: a gentleman, a carriage, and four posters. Miss Proudfoot, in agitation, had come herself to fetch Wright from the play-ground, calling her " darling." There was a sweetness and obsequiousness in her manner that was bewildering to the boarders. " Come, darling, your dear father is longing to see you!" And she gave her—unaccustomed luxury!—a glass of wine in the " study." For with school-boys and school-girls wine is the symbol of unutterable glory and even apotheosis. The chaise and four had spread the news; all was wonder and speculation. Miss Ventnor, the genteelest, and therefore the haughtiest, girl in the school, who thought the other girls mere " scum," whose sister had married a baronet, was awed and even curious. Our affectionate little jackal was in a tumult of delight. Cinderella's carriage and four could not have given much more joy. It betokened something good for her friend and idol.

In the parlour—chamber of horror or of joy, where severe or doting parents sat alternately— she was caught in the arms of her dear father. He was come to tell some great news. Their old cousin Panton had died, that rich, cross old man, and had left them a great fortune, and the beautiful castle by the river, which she could see from Miss Proudfoot's. They were now rolling in wealth, he and his little girl. At this the delicate girl slid off, and tossed back her head ; a curious look of exultation and pride came into her eyes. But they must both lose their dear old name, the name their mamma bore, and take another, which was quite as good, however.

"What matter," she said. "Who would care? but was she to be an heiress?"

"Yes."

"*And to have it all one day?*"

The new Sir Charles was disturbed at this question, and looked at her thoughtfully.

"Oh yes," he said with a smile, "after me, of course."

It was explained to her that the doctors found the air of St. Arthur's so good for her chest, she must remain a little longer under Miss Proudfoot's kind care. (How gladly would that lady, had she been permitted, have engraved that high testimonial on her programme: "In testimony of the healthy and salubrious air of her establishment, she is permitted proudly to refer to her distinguished pupil," &c.)

She drew back pettishly at this scheme, but it was shown to her that her stay was to be under quite altered conditions. She was to have a room to herself, *no lessons*, wine every day, doctors every week, to walk in the garden by herself or with any young friend whom she

preferred to keep her company. She reflected:
these bribes were not to be resisted. Miss Proudfoot had in the kindest manner given permission.
It was not mentioned then that Miss Proudfoot
had in the kindest manner also agreed to accept
double the usual payment, in return for these
privileges. She called it being a " parlour
boarder."

In future that name of Panton made the
whole glory of that white plastered house, with
" grounds" at the back overlooking the sea.
This was a kind of melodious bell, of gold or
other precious metal, on which the Principal
rang with never-flagging vigour triple and
quintuple bob majors on the subject of their
former illustrious pupil. They were privileged,
in their programmes, to refer to Miss Panton of
Panton Castle, who had received instruction in
the establishment. Reference was also permitted
to Sir Charles Panton of Panton. On Tuesdays
and Saturdays the pupils were accorded the kind
permission to take recreation in the grounds of
Panton Castle. To the parents and guardians

who had audience, the Misses Proudfoot, with most ingenious powers of apropos, contrived continually to draw in Sir Charles Panton and his daughter, met every doubt and objection with the same august names, and illustrated the progress of the studies, by scenes from the happy era when Miss Panton pursued her studies there; and a favourite tableau, as it were, often brought forward for the visitor, was one in which was grouped their illustrious pupil and that other young lady.

The change in Laura from this hour was scarcely conceivable. The new wealth of a sudden made her healthy, animated, and also inexpressibly arrogant. She rose into a sort of queenship, taking indescribable airs, which, alas for the sycophancy which repeats itself even at this small end of the worldly telescope, was accepted and endured by the school and its heads. But the worst feature was this: it was noted that she rather " dropped " her old friend and worshipper. This conspicuous ingratitude even surprised these other worldlings, for they had been saying to each other, "That now Wright (or Panton) would settle half her money upon Bailey." For a long time the clergyman's daughter herself could not see this strange conduct, marked as it was, and unmistakable even when she ran up to her idol at first, scarcely able to contain her delight, and was repulsed pettishly. For this and for many more instances of ungracious behaviour she could find excuses. It was so natural now that Laura should have much to think of; how could she think of her in this turn of fortune! Any over-looking was almost proper. When Miss Panton was seen "walking" with a new friend, suddenly elected to intimacy, no other than the young lady whose sister had married the baronet, she was not staggered. The public understood it perfectly: the new heiress was growing "fine;" but her young worshipper alone could not believe it, and would not. She would sooner disbelieve her senses or suppose that two and two made three, than accept the possibility of such an ungrateful change. She returned again and again, the other grew more and more arrogant; and from her new "nice" friend she was inseparable.

One day when they were engrossed in talk, and the future heiress was explaining what state they would have at Panton, how many horses she would keep, &c. (her favourite theme), Jessica approached humbly.

"Well, what is it ?" the other said, peevishly. "*I don't want you. You are always persecuting me.*"

Each of these nine words was a stab, each went deeper, until at last she could have given a scream. Some date a whole change in their system, their life itself, from a fit of sickness, from some shock ; and it was so with her. She retired almost reeling. What she could not see before she was forced to see now, as though some one were thrusting the flame of a candle close to her eyes. From that moment she shrank from Laura quite scared ; though she was still open to explanation of some kind. But the gap or chasm opened finally when the time came for the heiress to go away home, when she heard some of the pupils talking over every incident of the departure as though it were that of a royal personage. Her father, Sir Charles, had given her leave to choose a friend "whom she liked" from among the girls, to take home with her to amuse her during the vacation. This news produced the most tremendous excitement: some even said that Miss Proudfoot herself nourished faint hopes of being the selected companion, having performed prodigies in the way of obsequious adoration of her pupil, fawning on her, and plying her with praises of herself and of her "dear good father." The young girl, quite overset with her sudden turn of prosperity, did not care to restrain herself from any extravagance, and behaved with an amusing wantonness of arrogance, holding out hopes to some, but all the while pledged to her dear friend the baronet's sister-in-law. To others she made promises, but the faithful worshipping Jessica she passed over. When the morning came, and the carriage was waiting at the door, and the whole house was obsequiously gathered to see her go forth with her chosen companion, the baronet's sister-in-law, there was prodigious embracing all round; the clergyman's daughter standing at a distance, with a strange look upon her face, a kind of bewildered stare. It at last came to her turn, and with a sort of constraint Laura turned to bestow her parting accolade. But, to Miss Proudfoot's horror, Jessica, cold, stiff, and with a steady stare in her eyes, drew back.

"No," she said; "I cannot. I could not touch you—not for the whole world."

"As you please," said the other, coolly, and, getting into the carriage, drove away in her glory, the principals and scholars being inexpressibly shocked at this conduct. But from that hour all noticed a most singular change in the parson's daughter, who advanced at one stride half way on her path to womanhood. That discovery made her cold and hard, as she was before impulsive and affectionate; calculating and distrustful, a most "disagreeable creature," it was pronounced, but far more able to hold her own and get on in the world.

In the carriage which was taking Laura away that happy day there sat a young man of thirty, with very dark eyes, a forbidding, uninviting expression, which some would have called " a scowl." People would have passed him by without sympathy; but any one who came in contact with him in any trifling contention, say about a seat, went from him flushed and put out, and saying, "That ill-conditioned fellow!" This gentleman, a friend of her father's, was Mr. Dudley, a distant cousin, who came very often to the school to see his relation. It was known even to the girls that she did not relish these visits—" He was so dark and ugly," she said to her friends—and that every time he brought her presents she always seemed merely to endure him. Some of the girls, however, thought him "deeply piratical" and interesting, and also that he could smile sweetly.

But when she had thus left the school, and was established in all her splendour, as Miss

Panton, of Panton Castle, her proceedings became of profound interest to the neighbourhood. As the schoolgirl became a " young lady," it seemed to be her humour to exhibit that strange fitfulness and uncertainty of humour which wealth and indulgence had now made her character. It was seen also that Dudley was always about the place, either staying at the castle, or in the town, where he would appear in a small yacht at unexpected seasons. For him her father had a curious pity or partiality, and was ever saying, " Let us have that poor fellow Dudley here. He's your terrier dog, your worshipper." At which she would protest fretfully that she hated and loathed him, and would almost cry if the plan were persisted in. And yet, as a curious trait in her character, when her father at first would yield to her, thinking he was gratifying her, there would come another turn, and she would be fretful again at being taken at her word. To both he was very useful, almost necessary, because he was eager and willing. People wondered at this unmeaning alternation in so " ordinary " a girl, a girl, too, who had none of the redeeming virtues of spoiled or ill-regulated minds, namely, a wild and generous impulsiveness which hurries them into what is right. She, indeed, had more of the qualities which belong to the meaner animals; the uncertainty and spitefulness, in small matters, of the monkey. But there did at times come in her face a strange expression of desertion, of questing and seeking for help, which set every string in Dudley's heart a jangling.

He was half indignant with himself for this unmeaning partiality, and at first struggled to free himself; but, like a true spoiled child, when she saw he had nearly succeeded, she exerted her powers, and made him her slave again. It was about that era, when she had left school some three or four years, that she took a freak— for it was no more—of exhibiting this power in a most singular way. She had with her, on a visit, that baronet's sister-in-law, who had gone away from school with her, and whom she had treated in her favourite fitful way. This girl, it occurred to her one day, should marry Dudley. She set her heart on it; it was a new whim, and it should be done, just as she *should* have that horse or dress from her father, though it cost a thousand pounds. And to this task she set herself so petulantly and so desperately that Dudley saw he must gratify her, or else incur her bitter dislike. He was well off, the baronet's sister-in-law was not, and was eager to be married. To the surprise of his friends, to that of Sir Charles, and to the overflowing triumph of Miss Panton, this extraordinary marriage was actually brought about; though almost at once the new wife found that she had not her husband's heart, and, being impetuous and passionate, they separated within a few months, and Dudley came himself to tell Laura Panton the news.

"I hope you are satisfied with your handiwork," he said bitterly. "You can do no more, now—at least to *us !*"

She laughed lightly, and from that time—

about four years before this story begins—
treated him with more gentleness and toleration.
She seemed to consider him promoted to a
responsible station, and herself privileged to
consult him and make him useful. He seemed
to be quite happy in this mastiff-like office, and
came and went as he chose; and any new guest
at Panton often wondered at the dark, moody
and scowling man, whose eyes glared so, and
who spoke so little, save when he, the guest,
touched on *her*, and the scowling man became
eloquent. "Yes, look at her speaking face.
There is a whole world behind it. They think
here, because she will be so rich, and all that,
that she has no other title. I know her well,
and tell you there is a strange charm about this
girl which would attract if she had not a
farthing. Look, look at her now; see, as she
turns her face to the lamp! I cannot tell you
the effect on me." The guest cannot see it,
but thinks privately this is a very strange wild
creature of a man.

CHAPTER XVI.

DR. BAILEY was walking home by himself full of a sort of unusual excitement. The shops in the little new town were lighting up, lazy bands of sailors in the trim, dandy, yachting-dress, and with golden names of nymphs and goddesses on their hats, were strolling, lounging through the place, gathering at the Royal Yacht Tavern, and other sailors' houses, or were grouped in crowds in the centre of the street. Lights were twinkling everywhere, and converging to points at the end of long avenues. There was a hum and chatter of voices abroad, and yet with a general atmosphere of calm and rest, such as comes at the close of a day that has been busy and sultry. For this was a quiet June evening, and a June Saturday evening; and it was also all but the eve of the St. Arthur's-on-the-Sea Regatta, which was to commence on the Monday morning. The tiny harbour was already crowded with little black dashes surmounted with spiders'-web work. The yachts, which had come stealing in during the daytime, had now folded up their white wings for the night. Far off little white splashes could be made out on the purple-grey clouds of the horizon, fast becoming black, which were other yachts posting up, as it were, to reach an hotel, and get to bed comfortably. Down at the jetty's edge were other groups of seafaring men, sitting on benches or turned-over boats; whilst the most eloquent proclaimed the merits of "our craft," and boasted how the 'Diver' could beat the 'Mary Tanner' any day—names which figured in the yachting list as 'La Diva' and the 'Maritana.'

In accordance with the delightful vagabondage of yachting life, the St. Arthur's Regatta, at this time in its infancy, and "good-naturedly encour-aged," had drawn many noble strangers, noble creatures, the beauties of yacht creation, elegant symmetrical beings, to contend with each other; but, as with the beauty of the ball-room, no matter how fine the lines of her neck and figure, no matter what the Lapthornian milliner may have done for her, this year's belle is certain to give place to the new one of next year.

Sometimes, indeed, the existing queen will not give way without a petulant and spiteful struggle, disdaining to be vanquished by a mere chit of a thing just out. And once, perhaps, it is positively a pleasure to see an almost veteran stager like the 'Alarm' hold her own for season after season; lead off every ball triumphantly, and draw away all admirers from generations of younger rivals.

Down below could be seen indistinctly the huge 'Morna,' a boat of surprising reputation, and whose vast mainsail it took twenty men to get in. It was thought greedy on her part to come to snatch up the St. Arthur's prizes, and as nine o'clock came that night it was thought they were saved from her. But a little white speck began presently to enlarge and grow larger again, with such speed that the angry yachting men found themselves stamping fretfully, and saying, "that's her," or something like her. In a few minutes she was rolling in among them, her great sail like a vast cloud, which in a few moments more seemed to dissipate like a vapour, sending consternation and disgust among the yachtsmen on shore.

But well in the centre of the little haven reposed a handsome schooner, which lay haughtily, sullenly, and in the place of honour. She inspired respect, and belonged to the peerage of the craft. For from her bows floated the white flag, which translated, means R. Y. S., and over her bulwarks were seen little white dots, the clean and snowy uniform of her crew. She was known to be the 'Almandine,' one hundred and seventy, and belonging to Lord Formanton, though she had not the noble owner on board. His son, however, the Honourable George Conway, was there with a very distinguished nautical party, His Royal Highness the Prince of Saxe-

Gröningen, with Baron Bachmann, Lieutenant Bruce, and others. It was from this august craft that Doctor Bailey was returning on this fine June evening. He had gone on board to pay his respects, just as Her Majesty's consul goes on board at some foreign port. The German prince, indeed, from his imposing presence and manner, at first took him for some such public officer; but the doctor soon opened his pro- posals. He came, he said, to give them a cordial welcome to their regatta, and they would try to make everything as agreeable as possible during their stay. Two years ago, Count Lalandè, of the Paris club, looked in on them, and was delighted. He (Doctor Bailey) did everything for him. Now to-morrow was Sunday—a dull day. Would they so far honour him by coming to take a bit of lunch with him and Mrs. Bailey at The Beeches? They could walk about the grounds afterwards. Count Lalande had done so. Then, by the way, there was to be an appeal made by his unworthy lips for a meritorious charity—The Disabled Yachtsmen's Fund. In a place like this a little religion was no harm; but, of course, administered with discretion. No one had more experience among seamen than he had, but there was an art in insinuating the Word among them. He hoped Lord Formanton was in good health.

The Honourable George Conway and the German prince listened to these proposals. The truth was the foreigners rather shrank from the dull Sunday, and their pleasant wandering ways made a sudden introduction and acquaintance of ten minutes' ago quite familiar. They accepted the doctor's invitation as a matter of course, and promised to attend both lunch and sermon. The doctor strode home very happy and complacent, planning his lunch, looking at it fixedly, as though it were " laid " before him, up in the welkin. He stamped and creaked into his hall, letting the door slam behind him, then turning angrily as though some one else had done it. The contrast between his deferentially persuasive manner on board, and his loud, rough words of command in his own hall, was really startling.

"Here, come down—come here, quick!" A pale, fluttering, elderly little woman appeared before him, old-fashioned and pinched. She knew her inferior caste. "Hark, woman!" he said, "and see to this; and get those sluts below to do their work. They're coming to lunch, prince and all. So, see there's no bungling this time. Now, go along, and don't stand staring at *me!*"

Then this good doctor sat down to his desk to get ready for his sermon, which, indeed, was not difficult. He always had a few by him in stock on various models. There was what might be called the Almack's pattern—refined, oily, sweet-scented doctrine, that trickled over the edges of the pulpit, and flowed gently in the direction of the select pews. There was a good common-day pattern of the curate sort, which did well enough for the Sundays, at the dead level of the season, before Lady A. or Lord D. arrived. For these were "gala sermons." Finally, there were the "crowd sermons," when the place was very full, and quantity, if not quality, was present. On this night he took down a sermon preached one lucky Sunday when a royal duke had found himself there, and which "a little touching" could make just the thing for a German prince. Having got through this work he ordered his two women to write all out "legibly," and "see that they did so before going to bed." He went to his own, and slept there, whalelike in look, and making awful and cow-like sounds. He had an implied consciousness that he was sleeping a just man's sleep.

The harbour of St. Arthur's looked very bright on that Sunday morning. The yachts—pretty creatures, like pretty creatures on shore—had all their finery on; gay caps and ribbons, and snowy petticoats. The rival clubs flourished scarlet bunting at each other, as though offering a challenge. Tiny boats were rowing backward and forward; and from the 'Almandine' a barge, manned by six white-shirted rowers, was pulling in state for the stairs—alas! it was seen from the Royal Burgee, for the stairs of the Royal St. Arthur's. His Royal Highness the Prince of

Saxe - Gröningen, with the Honourable George Conway, ascended and walked to the church. At the door they were met by the vicar himself, who led them up the aisle, and shut them securely, and with a snap, into the large box of honour at the top. How happy would he have been, could he have thus treated all his friends of condition—above all, that wandering cabinet minister, who had been there for one day, and whom he might have never released till a promise of a bishopric had been extorted! It was crowded indeed: "hundreds had to be turned from the doors," as a gentleman of theatrical tastes said to his friend. All the leading people were present; and on a line with the august strangers were the baronet and his daughter, the heiress. The prince obtained much attention, far more than did the dull curate; and was observed to look round gaily and with curiosity, attending very little to his devotions: a fair sandy youth, perfectly self-possessed. But his companion excited more admiration. Even the devout noted how handsome and " thorough-bred " was the Honourable George Conway. This much may be said, that he was known among his friends as a "rock of good sense," though it was a little uncertain as to where he would finally fix that rock for good.

The doctor's heavy tread seemed to make the church quiver, and his gown, &c., clattered and flapped like the mainsail when going about. Indeed, it occurred to one of the Jack Tars that he was " carrying on " with too much canvas; and the pulpit creaked and strained as " that ere heavy gaff " was hoisted up. Then the doctor gave out his text, and made his Royal Highness of Saxe-Gröningen start with his loud round tones. There was nothing passionate in his appeal, and nothing threatening or "bullying like that ranter Buckley." It was a pleasant, kindly invitation to "Give, give"—the doctor pronounced it " gee-iff "—out of all that we could spare. We were *not* called on to abridge a single superfluity; on those in the higher stations pressed many claims and calls which seemed to those below luxuries. No; let us all give what we could spare. Again, the doctor drew an effective nautical picture. ."As in that contest, my brethren, which to-morrow will thrill every heart and kindle every eye, the proud skiff goes forth in all her beauty, drooping before the breeze, every sail set; suddenly comes on a storm—we are taken aback—we fly to the ropes, the hawsers —but it is too late. The squall is down on them—in a second the whole is a po-oor helpless wreck!" All the nautical men remarked confusion in this nautical description, and pointed out the mistake, and the mate of the 'Almandine' was heard to say, as he came out, that "that ere must have been a clumsy crew, mate," while a second, with some vehemence, "that that ere skipper had best stick to his own business, seeing as how he didn't know a rope from a hawser!" while a third, affecting to see an allusion to the 'Morna,' said, "It was unfair for a parson to be prejudicing the race. But she'd beat in spite of all the black gentry that ever rode in a pulpit."

On coming out the doctor received compliments from the distinguished party. At the same moment a tall good-looking man, in a yachting surtout, came up. He had a hard face, and was bald. He seemed as though he had "lived a great deal," and was greeted by the young man.

"Hallo, Dudley, what you coming to church?" he said good-humouredly — "Prince, let me introduce Colonel Dudley."

The doctor was beside them already, an improvised equerry. The crowd of fashion lingered reluctantly, and the doctor's open carriage was waiting.

"The Prince and Mr. Conway are coming up to lunch," said the doctor, in a voice that could be heard beyond the church. "If you will come, Colonel Dudley——"

The other was looking back to the church door, expecting some one to come out; then, without answering, broke away, as it were, and went to join the baronet and his daughter.

The doctor "blew" a little, and got red. "A man of no manners, as you know, Mr. Conway," he said. " Lives altogether a vagabond life."

" Oh I see," said Mr. Conway, with interest; " those must be the people he is always talking about."

" *You* see how it is, Mr. Conway," said the doctor. " A true Formanton, sir. Yes, a vulgar longing after the heiress. Will you get in, Prince ?"

" But, your daughter and family ?" said the Prince, politely.

" Oh, pooh !" said the doctor, as if to the servants ; " they've got home someway, never fear."

The three gentlemen got in, and the carriage drove away to The Beeches. The doctor talked all the time, and described—for he knew the country as well as a " lecturer" does his pano- rama. Sometimes Mr. Conway questioned him, and seemed to reflect on what he said.

" Curious," he said, after a pause, " Dudley's turning up here. We last saw him on the Nile."

" Dear, dear ! " said the doctor, bursting with enthusiasm. " There are wheels, you see, dozens of 'em within each other. That's his cousin, our heiress, the future baronetess, as my son calls her."

" But he's married," said Conway, gravely : " it seems strange, does it not ? "

" My dear sir, there's no being up to men of that sort. He quite hangs about Panton—a cousin, you know. And she, the wife, was such a strange, ill-regulated, dreadful person."

" Here we are ! " said the doctor several times, almost at each sweep of the avenue. " Here we are," is always accepted by the person to whom it is addressed with a sort of surprise and gratitude, though he is already in possession of the information. At the hall door, the doctor said " Here we are," for the last time, and got out.

CHAPTER XVII.

THE LUNCH.

Dr. Bailey led his two guests in, and as he did so, a young girl came to meet them. "This is my daughter Jessica," said the doctor, scarcely with the importance that he would have said "This is our front drawing-room."

It occurred to Mr. Conway, and to the German Prince, what a "strange girl this was," what a quickness and spirit in the motion of her eye and head, what a character there was. She seemed to challenge them, inquire what was in their thoughts, to colour as she read those thoughts. She was about one-and-twenty, and was a girl that could make her own way.

"An invasion!" said the Prince, in good English; "an invasion, Miss Bailey."

"Not at all," she said. "Papa asked you, and we are so glad."

Smart, thought Conway, or she thinks herself so. A pity. He would give her another chance.

"Sunday is so dull in harbour," he began, and paused.

A really smart girl, he thought, could not let this chance go, but must reply, "And Mr. Conway only comes to us to avoid the dull harbour." But instead, her eyes dropped suddenly, and she said :

"It was very kind of you, indeed." Mr. Conway was a remarkably interesting man, and had a legion of lady admirers.

"Oh, come in and sit down," said the doctor, impatiently. "Go, child, and hurry your mother; these gentlemen are hungry, and don't keep us waiting. Come in here, Prince, you shall taste my cognac: finest in the three kingdoms." It will be seen that the Reverend Doctor Bailey was something of an under-bred man. With him it was all "his" and "my"; a red, swollen pampered " my " ; " my house, my furniture, my servants, my women," &c. All these elements were to his service, honour, and glory.

The Prince said, perhaps a little maliciously : " Will you not allow us the pleasure of presenting our homage to Mrs. Bailey ? "

" Oh, to be sure, to be sure," said the doctor ; " she will be here presently. These servants of ours, I can tell you, Prince——"

" She your servant ? " said Mr. Conway. " Oh, I see now," he added, correcting himself.

" Ah, here is lunch ! " said the doctor, as the folding door was thrown open. " For once Mrs. Bailey has not been an hour late." The doctor began to stride. But the Prince stopped to offer his arm to Miss Jessica. " You are coming in to lunch, are you not ? This is not surely after dinner, when the gentlemen drink alone ? "

The girl hesitated.

" God bless me," said her father, " you are always getting up some fuss ! Don't let us stand upon the order of our going, Prince. Come in."

But the latter, with great ceremoniousness, offered his arm, with a low foreign bend and bow, to the young lady. The doctor began to blow and walked behind, raising his hands impatiently.

The lady of the house stole down after they were seated. And the ceremonious Prince had risen and was bowing, and offering his chair. The doctor "blew," and "phewed" again, and remained with his soup-ladle poised. He conveyed the idea that he would have liked to have used it, say on the side of a human head divine, and for quite another purpose than for helping soup.

She scarcely spoke, but Mr. Conway noticed that her daughter determined, as of set purpose, that she should be noticed and have her place.

"I hope we shall see a great deal of you," said the doctor, lubricating his lips with rich gravy. "Here—help the Prince! Now you must, you really must come often; you know the way here."

Conway, who was a perfect gentleman, seemed to take a pleasure in bringing forward Mrs. Bailey.

"But what can *you* say to such an arrangement? Two boisterous sailors bursting in, and taking possession of the house! No, indeed, we must think of you."

"What folly!" said the doctor; "don't mind them. What have they to do with it? Come when you like!"

"What have they to do with it?" repeated Conway, with assumed astonishment. "Surely, Doctor Bailey, ladies have to do with all that is worth anything in this world. I am afraid (and you must not think me rude for telling you so) your own unaided attraction would not go far."

This, though said with the air of a joke, was more in earnest than in joke, and the doctor began to blow and phew a good deal, as his habit was when there was something he did not quite understand.

"And we find Dudley here," said Mr. Conway. "I have hardly got over that surprise yet."

" An ill-conditioned man, Mr. Conway, very much so ; he is not the sort of thing, you know ; and really, when you consider my position, I ought scarcely to tolerate a man situated as he is."

" Oh ! you have told us that," said Conway, very coldly. " We are in possession of the scandal. You know Miss Panton, our heiress here ? " he said, turning abruptly to Jessica. " Every one adores her."

Instantly he saw a bit of dramatic action in her face ; two or three shades of opposite feelings seemed to drift across it, much as they had seen cloud shadows gliding across their mainsail.

" Yes, I do know her," she answered steadily ; " but I do not adore her ; and I don't think that everybody does, and "—this after slow pausings—" she is much too rich."

" I saw her at the church to-day, and she seemed behind the rail of a cash-office."

Jessica was first going to say something, then something else ; then seemed to check herself, and said a third thing eagerly and fervently.

"I do not like her, and I cannot, though I have tried. Perhaps the reason is that she does not like me."

"What folly you talk, child!" said her father, roughly. "I assure you, Mr. Conway, she is charming : all that estate for miles—you can see it from the top window of this house—is hers. Beautiful house, and all entailed on herself, family jewels, savings. Oh, I assure you she is very charming. Jessica talks without thinking."

There was some scorn in Mr. Conway's face, and Miss Jessica, who was as quickly intelligent as she was quickly sensitive, saw it there. It made her move impatiently in her chair.

"What! an estate for miles, savings, family jewels!" repeated Mr. Conway, quietly, and without any appearance of sarcasm. "She must be beautiful!"

"A really fine woman!" said the doctor, pleased. "Oh, there's no doubt about the money."

"It's wonderful!" continued Mr. Conway, as if ruminating; "and I have a conviction she must be good and pious and charitable, and have every virtue.   Am I right?"

"You are, indeed, Mr. Conway—a true man of judgment, I see."

"You are making fun of us, Mr. Conway," said Miss Jessica, in so excited a tone that the German Prince, working at his food with vigour, looked up with surprise.   "You are trying to draw us out, rustic people—you who have travelled about and seen the world.   Oh! it is great sport—you who have——"

"JESSICA!" her fathered thundered, his fork in the air.

"See, he can't deny it.   He has too much truth.   No," she added, her eyes questioning him, "you will not!"   He was a little confused. "She is beautiful because she has money; she is good for the same reason.   Papa was entrapped into saying it."

"Oh, come, come, now, do stop," said the clergyman, very hotly and roughly; "there is always something of this sort.   You mustn't be getting into this kind of business, putting out our little lunch in this way. It's really too much. I won't have it in my house. Really, you ought to beg Mr. Conway's pardon."

Jessica stood up, and repeated slowly, " Beg Mr. Conway's pardon !" She then gave a scornful look all round, and walked towards the door.

The Prince had jumped up to open it. " The ladies leaving us already ?" he said, with a foreigner's tact. " These cruel English customs of yours !"

Mr. Conway rose, too, but said nothing.

Doctor Bailey was quite "put out"; his lips inflated and collapsed again. " I don't know *what* you will think of us ?" he said; "she is self-willed, you know, and really I must have her taught control and——"

" We must not spoil this good wine with any scolding of Miss Bailey," said the other. " For my part, I admire nature and spirit. Apropos of the heiress, though we own to being curious — every one *is* about the sights and shows, lions and lionesses of a district——"

"Most natural, most natural," obsequiously said the doctor.

"The contrast between her and your daughter I can quite imagine. I know nothing more intolerable than the perpetual challenge of wealth, a sort of concrete arrogance, the buying your way, as it were, buying the *pas*, too, every moment. I know it would grate on me, and fret me to death."

The doctor did not follow this refining at all. The idea of money "grating" or "fretting" to death! At that moment he formed the conclusion that the Honourable Mr. Conway was "a poor creature full of young ladies' talk." "I don't know about that," he said, "but I wish my son Tom had her."

Then the gentlemen talked of the baronet himself, who had left his card at the yacht, and again came back the curious relation of Colonel Dudley.

"I have known that sort of shepherd's dog attendance," said Conway, "before now. A man is unhappy in his own home, and he finds a soothing feeling in the company of some congenial face. He asks no more; to breathe the same air is enough. He would not care if it went on so for years. I dare say he travels about with them as one of the retinue. It tranquillises him."

"Precisely, but a great drawback to her advancement, you know. He scowls at every man that comes up."

"And if one had a son," said Conway, smiling, "most unpleasant. But one should never mind his scowls."

Doctor Bailey was presently showing his visitors the "grounds" and gardens. "My hothouse," "my greenhouse," "my gardens," his general stately "my," which was really the point of what he was exhibiting. This was for the German Prince, who resigned himself with the sad dreamy politeness of his country. Conway went to the drawing-room.

Jessica, in a pale green striped dress, was walking up and down with stately pacing. She seemed to be talking haughtily to some invisible companion; not to her mother, who was in the more congenial "housekeeper's-room," the locality where she would have asked any one to " Come live with me and be my love."

There are some characters " drifting " about this world, sometimes being " kicked about," which are mere fragments, each with the serried outline of a fracture. By some rare chance, both come together one day, and fit to a nicety in one piece. Had these two, Conway and Jessica, thus joined unexpectedly, and did both know it?

" You were angry with me," he said, deferentially, "and I have come to beg pardon. I did two things which fretted you; I wanted respect to your father, and praised up that rich woman who is as distasteful to me as she is to you."

Jessica smiled and put out her hand. " Indeed I am not angry, and I am not ashamed of myself. My father says I disgrace him everywhere, and that I am pettish."

" You must let me see you, then, under better auspices," said Conway, gravely. " Otherwise I may run the risk of taking away an unfavourable impression."

"Indeed!" said Jessica, scornful again. "And that is your gracious pleasure. Then I tell you candidly, Mr. Conway, I am *not* sorry, and I do not think it good taste to sneer at a gentleman at his own table, and before others. Now!"

Conway coloured, and was angry. He had quite mistaken this young lady.

"You are too severe for me," he said, "and really beat me to the ground."

She made no answer, and swept out just as the doctor and the German entered. The doctor blew and phewed, and muttered, " Oh, unbearable! such behaviour!" but the young lady did not return. Before the two gentlemen drove away it was arranged that the doctor and his family should come and see the 'Almandine,' and take the opportunity of there being fireworks on the following nights, when a little supper could be "knocked up."

"Oh, I shall come, certainly," the doctor said,

eagerly. "So glad to know you are better. We have all heard of his Lordship, your good father, and I will take the liberty of asking you to mention that you have seen *me*, the Vicar of St. Arthur's. He will recollect a little correspondence we had two years ago. A finer, nobler character does not exist in this broad England of ours."

Conway seemed to convey surprise at this large statement. "My father is a most excellent man," he said, in his quiet way; "I shall give him your message."

"Do, do, my dear Mr. Conway," the doctor went on, as though he were preaching. "He will know me. I wanted him to take the chair for us down here for The Disabled Yachtsmen. He was busy, I suppose, so we got Lord Rufus Cocker. Good-bye—*good*-bye."

Wine at lunch was like kindling the furnace fires for the doctor, so all the cranks and machinery were working, the steam blowing off, and all the oils oozing out.

"We shall write formally to the ladies," said

Conway, "and you can tell them. In the mean time——"

"Oh, she never goes," the doctor said, waving off his wife, "that sort of thing don't suit her. And, as for Jessica—if you wish——"

"Oh, but my good sir," said Conway, decisively, "this must be understood. The rule of the Yacht is to admit no single gentlemen on these gala occasions. I assure you she is inflexible in that."

This seemed like bantering, but there was a blunt and malicious decision about Conway's manner that told the doctor that the Yacht might not be "at home" for him if he came without his wife.

CHAPTER XVIII.

A HOLIDAY.

MONDAY morning. A bright, fresh day with
a distant stiff breeze, which every now and again
caused a dark purple frown to pass over the sea
very far away. The old sailors said this meant
nothing, that "afore noon" it would be all right,
with a "good sailin' breeze." The harbour
seemed to have half the air of a nautical flower-
show—so many sails were fluttering in a sort of
negligée toilette. A few more of these elegant
ladies had dropped in during the night, and for
the first race it was known that at least ten
would start. Of course the shabby, greedy
'Morna' was among them. "Scandalous,"
many a mariner, his hands deep in his pockets,
muttered. Little boats shot about the harbour

zigzag, like gad-flies, and the Royal St. Arthur's and the Royal Burgee in full uniform, and stuck over with innumerable flags, affected a sort of harmony for that day only.

A gunboat from one of the great ports was hovering undecidedly outside the harbour; the lieutenant was being pulled ashore; but even that "rubbishing fellow" went straight for the stairs of the Royal St. Arthur's. The terraces of both clubs were covered with gentlemen in short jackets and caps, and using glasses, with quite a quarter-deck air. The start was early: about nine o'clock. From the commodore's yacht came the gun, and the row of racers were "round" in a second, and gliding away out of the harbour. The selfish cutter took her time, and rather "lounged" out. She had on her racing suit, and when she got up her "balloon" sails, seemed to swell like the snowy feathers of a huge swan. There was the local crack boat, known indifferently to the sailors as the 'Nigh-a-Bee,' sometimes as the 'Knee-Oby,' but which in Hunt's List was the 'Niobe,' 35; W. C.

Jephson, owner. This gentleman could hardly contain his disgust as he looked at the intruder, who was aristocratic R.Y.S., while he was only R. St. A.Y.C. There she was, a smart coquettish, thoroughbred thing, shooting out of the harbour before all the rest; but, " of course," there was the huge hulking ' Morna ' rolling carelessly on behind, and getting up another tremendous sail, though in the most leisurely manner. The rest went on their way in straggling order—here, there, and everywhere, leaning over, awry, stiffly upright, or flying along half arching over, like graceful skaters. The course was one of many miles; in a short time the graceful craft were afar off, no more than a few yellowish specks dotted about, and the spectators on shore had done with them for nearly the whole day.

The ' Almandine,' like some fastidious guards-man, seemed to think the affair " a bore," and disdained to take the trouble of racing at all. She lay in the centre of the harbour, tranquilly, as if reposing on a sort of watery sofa, full of charming languor. Round her circulated innumerable gay pleasure-boats, all parasols and bright ribbons. Towards two o'clock, the terraces of the Royal St. Arthur's and of the Royal Burgee became crowded, and the band of the Sixth (Prince Regent's Own), one circle of legs and jackets, with caps at about the sloping angle of a roof, played "selections" under the direction of Herr Spoffman. They had been brought by special train. The Royal St. Arthur's were giving a *déjeuner à la fourchette*, in the boat-house, at four o'clock. The commodore and vice-commodore of the Royal Burgee were, almost perforce, invited; and the members of the Royal Burgee, though they hated it, still spoke with pride of the invitation, and told each other at the house "that the commodore and vice ditto were over at St. Arthur's."

As the day wore on, the excitement increased, and the crowds gathered more thickly on the pier. Special trains began to arrive from neighbouring manufacturing towns. On the jetty and pier were the usual "Fair" supernumeraries; fellows shooting for nuts, the

roulettes, the carts of spruce and ginger-beer.
These familiars take the race-course and the
regatta on their circuit indifferently. The
Cheap Jacks lectured. But suddenly amongst
the motley group appeared an open carriage, with
a very large gentleman in a large hat—a bright
girl beside him—who was calling out, in a loud
voice, "Don't stop the way, please, stand aside
—we are in a hurry!" No wonder Doctor
Bailey was eager, for he could actually hear the
voice of "that low Buckley" close by, who was
in the midst of a ring on a granite stone, asking
a large crowd whether "their timbers were
secure and well caulked; whether their ropes
were taut, and were they ready to mount the
ship's side, up the glorious gangway of faith,
and step on the quarter-deck of the resur-
rection?"

Seeing faces turning away from him at the
sound of carriage-wheels, Mr. Buckley went on.
"Is *that* the way to put out on the sea of
righteousness, in purple and fine linen, and,"
with a slight confusion of metaphor, "rolling

in one's carriage? Is it by going down to riot, and drink, and eat, and be filled, and make merry, like the swine, that the God-fearing mariner fits himself for his work?" &c.

Thus did the low Buckley make the doctor serve as a text and homily. What did the latter care? There he was, getting down at the door of the Royal St. Arthur's, and striding in with his daughter on his arm. "Keep back these people, policeman," he said. "There's really no getting into one's own house. Sir —he has come, I suppose? eh, Bowles? Seen the Prince about?"

Thus he passed in, pushing his way with many a "Let me pass, please! People should move on, and not crowd in the doors." Miss Jessica's lips were contracted, and to other people she looked as overbearing as her father. Out on the terrace, they came among the gay company where the Prince Regent's own were drumming and clattering the eternal 'Trovatore,' with infinite noise.

In a moment Mr. Conway was beside them,

and was seized, swallowed up in the vast greeting of the tremendous doctor, who was himself family, daughter, wife, all, and spoke for all. With a quiet inattention, Mr. Conway put him aside and welcomed Jessica. She was all interest, all excitement. She had been looking out for him eagerly, as he saw. The doctor became of a sudden submerged in business, calling out, looking for some one.

"Where's Colman? Send him here, do! Has Sir Charles come? Here, ma'am, be good enough, do. Don't crowd about the passage; people can't get in or out," &c.

He was now in the boat-house, looking after the *déjeuner;* now out of the boat-house, looking after the great people, and all the while, not unnaturally, in a very great heat.

"I am so glad to meet you," said Jessica. "What you thought of me I do not know. But there are people who try and 'draw out' my father, as they call it, and I thought——"

"You thought I could be so ill-bred, so ungentlemanly?" said Conway, colouring.

"I did," said she, fearlessly. "I tell the truth always, though you may despise me, and make yourself my enemy for ever."

"Well, you are independent, like myself. I should have made the same answer, I suspect. And I like you the better for telling me this. Look here; who comes by? You will tell me all the notables."

It was the doctor, and a short, spare, wiry, grey gentleman, in a white coat and blue tie, and with a tall young lady on his arm. She was dressed to perfection, and a certain good taste about her made her face handsome. It was Laura the HEIRESS, and though the majority there were above everything mean, yet the presence of so much wealth unconsciously fluttered them all, and numbers of necks and heads were twisted and craned "to get a good view." People even reverently made way and drew back with an awe they were ashamed of, but could not resist. If all were saints, money must force this homage. The doctor was their grand chamberlain. "See here, Sir Charles. That's the

'Almandine,' Lord Formanton's, you know, fine vessel. I had the son and his friend, the Prince of Saxe-Gröningen, to lunch with me. Most gentlemanly fellow. Ah! by the way, Sir Charles, here he is. Conway, allow me. Sir Charles Panton—Miss Panton."

Conway, perfect gentleman as he was, could give a rebuke, or be insolent even, with his face. He conveyed by his cold bow that he had not desired this introduction, and conveyed it to all parties concerned.

" I hope Doctor Bailey," he said, turning to Jessica, " will not ask me to make any more acquaintances. I make it a point to be disagreeable, and a Miss Mammon I *never* can stand."

" I am delighted," said Jessica, enthusiastically. " My father thinks them the greatest people in the world, and is always asking them, or wishing to be asked by them. You saw how she looked at me. She is empress over this part of the country. But I am not under her, and disdain her rule, and would die before I would submit to her. And she knows it."

"How you and I shall agree!" said Conway. "It is refreshing to hear such independence. I am independent, too, of all the world, except of a certain good but rather ambitious person, whose name is Formanton."

"Oh, your father?" said she.

"Yes. My poor mother, last and only one of all my friends, left me to him. I am his while he lives, as much as a serf used to be in Russia. But for this I should have done something. As it is, I have been leading an actor's life, instead of doing something useful. Now I have grown old, and the best part of life is gone. But I have made a promise, and must stick to it. 'Stick to it!' Is not that a refined speech? Even in English, where I used to be rather 'nice.' You see the decay?"

It must have been time for the *déjeuner*, for Doctor Bailey was bustling people about, and giving loud orders, causing angry faces to be turned round as he stood on dresses and roughly pushed past ladies. He was always hot and angry when he stood on a lady's dress, or dragged it from her waist.

"*Such* things! A man can't walk. I really *must* ask you, ma'am, to stand out of the way. No one can get by."

"Rude bear!" "Savage!" were the whispered rejoinders. There was another lady of rank present, whom the doctor himself had described as " a broken-down honourable," whom he was obliged to "take in," and he gave out orders right and left to others, dragging this partner about, and clutching at young men. "Here, you—get somebody and take 'em in." Then his eye fell on Miss Panton, and he seized Mr. Conway and eagerly "hauled" him to her side. As for his own daughter, what did it matter what became of *her?* Conway, now that fate was inexorable, offered himself for duty with perfect complacency, But he could see the unconcealed dissatisfaction, the open colour, of the lady he was thus obliged to leave. This sort of character, clear as crystal, which disdained to conceal, was really new to him, and quite inviting.

With his new companion he was quite a different person. He became the conventional gentleman of parties and amusements, asked with apparent interest as to her balls and parties, and talked in the usual personal way of his own movements. One thing she saw clearly, he was not in the least impressed by her acknowledged sovereignty.

"I see you know those Baileys," she said, pettishly. "Very pushing people, are they not?" He had never met so fretted a voice.

"I like *her*," said Mr. Conway, with an affected warmth. "She is charmingly natural, and full of honesty. But to be pitied with that intrusive father, who should have been chamberlain at a little German court, not an English clergyman."

"I know little of them," said she, haughtily. "Of course we exchange visits, and that sort of thing, but I do not wish to go beyond it."

"So I have heard," said Conway, smiling. "They have told me already that Miss Panton is queen of this country for miles round. They speak with distending eyes, and gaping mouths, of her vast wealth, and gold, and jewels. I am sure it must amuse you. But these poor people can't help it, you know. It is their nature."

" And these people I suppose have been telling you all this? That is their nature also, I suppose?"

" These people?" repeated Mr. Conway, wishing "to take her down" a little. "Oh, Dr. Bailey and Miss Bailey. I see, I am getting on the thin ice. You know, a stranger, such as I may call myself, for I have been away for six or seven years, cannot be, nor is he expected to be, posted up in the little vendettas of a place like this."

The pettish look she gave him, gave him pleasure afterwards to think of.

" *I* a vendetta with them! I repeat they are outside our circle. It is barely an acquaintance. You might as well say I have a vendetta with that sailor there."

" No doubt," said he, gravely ; "and my stay in this place has been only a day or so long. But as a mere fact of general experience your illustration does not hold. In plays, you know, the wicked lord often takes a horrid and unmeaning dislike to his virtuous tenant in a red waistcoat."

All this while two sullen eyes had been bent on them from the opposite side of the room, and he thus heard a voice beside him, "Red waistcoats and virtuous tenants! Do you hear this, Conway? Let me warn you," he added to her, "he has got well furnished with all the refinements and metaphysics. I know him; and with these little smart things he makes himself interesting. I know you of old, my dear friend."

"No you do not," said the other, coolly. "That is much too highly coloured an account of our acquaintance. Pardon me if I am wrong, but you know very little about me, Dudley. Now, Miss Panton, come into this place. I am sure you must be tired, and perhaps hungry."

There was a vast clatter of plates, knives and forks, and champagne explosion. The natives of the district were not generally accustomed to such rich and gratuitous entertainments. They flung themselves on the banquet with something like ravenousness. It was hard to hear a neighbour's voice through it all.

END OF VOL I.

www.ingramcontent.com/pod-product-compliance
Lightning Source LLC
Chambersburg PA
CBHW031153120726
47905CB00006B/1931